Henry James

Henry James OM (15 April 1843 – 28 February 1916) was an American-British author regarded as a key transitional figure between literary realism and literary modernism, and is considered by many to be among the greatest novelists in the English language. He was the son of Henry James Sr. and the brother of renowned philosopher and psychologist William James and diarist Alice James.

He is best known for a number of novels dealing with the social and marital interplay between émigré Americans, English people, and continental Europeans. Examples of such novels include The Portrait of a Lady, The Ambassadors, and The Wings of the Dove. His later works were increasingly experimental. In describing the internal states of mind and social dynamics of his characters, James often made use of a style in which ambiguous or contradictory motives and impressions were overlaid or juxtaposed in the discussion of a character's psyche. (Source: Wikipedia)

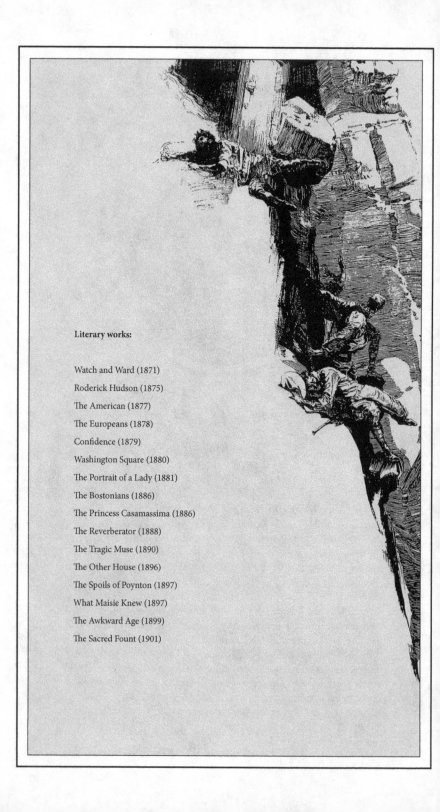

Literary works:

Watch and Ward (1871)

Roderick Hudson (1875)

The American (1877)

The Europeans (1878)

Confidence (1879)

Washington Square (1880)

The Portrait of a Lady (1881)

The Bostonians (1886)

The Princess Casamassima (1886)

The Reverberator (1888)

The Tragic Muse (1890)

The Other House (1896)

The Spoils of Poynton (1897)

What Maisie Knew (1897)

The Awkward Age (1899)

The Sacred Fount (1901)

THE
WORKS
OF
HENRY JAMES

VOL. 15 (OF 36)

SOME SHORT STORIES
THE ALTAR OF THE DEAD

An Imprint of Moon Classics LLC

A Wholly Owned Subsidary of Queenior LLC

A Melodragon Company

First Printing: 2020

ISBN 978-1-6627-1576-1 (Paperback)

ISBN 978-1-6627-1577-8 (Hardcover)

Published by Moon Classics

www.moonclassics.com

Contents

THE
WORKS
OF
HENRY JAMES
VOL. 15 (OF 36)

SOME SHORT STORIES

BROOKSMITH

We are scattered now, the friends of the late Mr. Oliver Offord; but whenever we chance to meet I think we are conscious of a certain esoteric respect for each other. "Yes, you too have been in Arcadia," we seem not too grumpily to allow. When I pass the house in Mansfield Street I remember that Arcadia was there. I don't know who has it now, and don't want to know; it's enough to be so sure that if I should ring the bell there would be no such luck for me as that Brooksmith should open the door. Mr. Offord, the most agreeable, the most attaching of bachelors, was a retired diplomatist, living on his pension and on something of his own over and above; a good deal confined, by his infirmities, to his fireside and delighted to be found there any afternoon in the year, from five o'clock on, by such visitors as Brooksmith allowed to come up. Brooksmith was his butler and his most intimate friend, to whom we all stood, or I should say sat, in the same relation in which the subject of the sovereign finds himself to the prime minister. By having been for years, in foreign lands, the most delightful Englishman any one had ever known, Mr. Offord had in my opinion rendered signal service to his country. But I suppose he had been too much liked—liked even by those who didn't like IT—so that as people of that sort never get titles or dotations for the horrid things they've *NOT* done, his principal reward was simply that we went to see him.

Oh we went perpetually, and it was not our fault if he was not overwhelmed with this particular honour. Any visitor who came once came again; to come merely once was a slight nobody, I'm sure, had ever put upon him. His circle therefore was essentially composed of habitués, who were habitués for each other as well as for him, as those of a happy salon should be. I remember vividly every element of the place, down to the intensely Londonish look of the grey opposite houses, in the gap of the white curtains of the high windows, and the exact spot where, on a particular afternoon, I put down my tea-cup for Brooksmith, lingering an instant, to gather it up as if he were plucking a flower. Mr. Offord's drawing-room was indeed Brooksmith's garden, his pruned and tended human parterre, and if we all flourished there and grew well in our places it was largely owing to his supervision.

Many persons have heard much, though most have doubtless seen little, of the famous institution of the salon, and many are born to the depression of knowing that this finest flower of social life refuses to bloom where the English tongue is spoken. The explanation is usually that our women have not the skill to cultivate it—the art to direct through a smiling land, between suggestive shores, a sinuous stream of talk. My affectionate, my pious memory of Mr. Offord contradicts this induction only, I fear, more insidiously to confirm it. The sallow and slightly smoked drawing-room in which he spent so large a portion of the last years of his life certainly deserved the distinguished name; but on the other hand it couldn't be said at all to owe its stamp to any intervention throwing into relief the fact that there was no Mrs. Offord. The dear man had indeed, at the most, been capable of one of those sacrifices to which women are deemed peculiarly apt: he had recognised—under the influence, in some degree, it is true, of physical infirmity—that if you wish people to find you at home you must manage not to be out. He had in short accepted the truth which many dabblers in the social art are slow to learn, that you must really, as they say, take a line, and that the only way as yet discovered of being at home is to stay at home. Finally his own fireside had become a summary of his habits. Why should he ever have left it?—since this would have been leaving what was notoriously pleasantest in London, the compact charmed cluster (thinning away indeed into casual couples) round the fine old last-century chimney-piece which, with the exception of the remarkable collection of miniatures, was the best thing the place contained. Mr. Offord wasn't rich; he had nothing but his pension and the use for life of the somewhat superannuated house.

When I'm reminded by some opposed discomfort of the present hour how perfectly we were all handled there, I ask myself once more what had been the secret of such perfection. One had taken it for granted at the time, for anything that is supremely good produces more acceptance than surprise. I felt we were all happy, but I didn't consider how our happiness was managed. And yet there were questions to be asked, questions that strike me as singularly obvious now that there's nobody to answer them. Mr. Offord had solved the insoluble; he had, without feminine help—save in the sense that ladies were dying to come to him and that he saved the lives of several—established a salon; but I might have guessed that there was a method in his madness, a law in his success. He hadn't hit it off by a mere fluke. There was an art in it all, and how was the art so hidden? Who indeed if it came to that was the occult artist? Launching this inquiry the other day I had already got hold of the tail of my reply. I was helped by the very wonder of some of the conditions that came back to me—those that used to seem as natural as sunshine in a fine climate.

How was it for instance that we never were a crowd, never either too many or too few, always the right people *with* the right people—there must really have been no wrong people at all—always coming and going, never sticking fast nor overstaying, yet never popping in or out with an indecorous familiarity? How was it that we all sat where we wanted and moved when we wanted and met whom we wanted and escaped whom we wanted; joining, according to the accident of inclination, the general circle or falling in with a single talker on a convenient sofa? Why were all the sofas so convenient, the accidents so happy, the talkers so ready, the listeners so willing, the subjects presented to you in a rotation as quickly foreordained as the courses at dinner? A dearth of topics would have been as unheard of as a lapse in the service. These speculations couldn't fail to lead me to the fundamental truth that Brooksmith had been somehow at the bottom of the mystery. If he hadn't established the salon at least he had carried it on. Brooksmith in short was the artist!

We felt this covertly at the time, without formulating it, and were conscious, as an ordered and prosperous community, of his even-handed justice, all untainted with flunkeyism. He had none of that vulgarity—his touch was infinitely fine. The delicacy of it was clear to me on the first occasion my eyes rested, as they were so often to rest again, on the domestic revealed, in the turbid light of the street, by the opening of the house-door. I saw on the spot that though he had plenty of school he carried it without arrogance—he had remained articulate and human. *L'Ecole Anglaise* Mr.

Offord used laughingly to call him when, later on, it happened more than once that we had some conversation about him. But I remember accusing Mr. Offord of not doing him quite ideal justice. That he wasn't one of the giants of the school, however, was admitted by my old friend, who really understood him perfectly and was devoted to him, as I shall show; which doubtless poor Brooksmith had himself felt, to his cost, when his value in the market was originally determined. The utility of his class in general is estimated by the foot and the inch, and poor Brooksmith had only about five feet three to put into circulation. He acknowledged the inadequacy of this provision, and I'm sure was penetrated with the everlasting fitness of the relation between service and stature. If HE had been Mr. Offord he certainly would have found Brooksmith wanting, and indeed the laxity of his employer on this score was one of many things he had had to condone and to which he had at last indulgently adapted himself.

I remember the old man's saying to me: "Oh my servants, if they can live with me a fortnight they can live with me for ever. But it's the first fortnight that tries 'em." It was in the first fortnight for instance that Brooksmith had had to learn that he was exposed to being addressed as "my dear fellow" and "my poor child." Strange and deep must such a probation have been to him, and he doubtless emerged from it tempered and purified. This was written to a certain extent in his appearance; in his spare brisk little person, in his cloistered white face and extraordinarily polished hair, which told of responsibility, looked as if it were kept up to the same high standard as the plate; in his small clear anxious eyes, even in the permitted, though not exactly encouraged, tuft on his chin. "He thinks me rather mad, but I've broken him in, and now he likes the place, he likes the company," said the old man. I embraced this fully after I had become aware that Brooksmith's main characteristic was a deep and shy refinement, though I remember I was rather puzzled when, on another occasion, Mr. Offord remarked: "What he likes is the talk—mingling in the conversation." I was conscious I had never seen Brooksmith permit himself this freedom, but I guessed in a moment that what Mr. Offord alluded to was a participation more intense than any speech could have represented—that of being perpetually present on a hundred legitimate pretexts, errands, necessities, and breathing the very atmosphere of criticism, the famous criticism of life. "Quite an education, sir, isn't it, sir?" he said to me one day at the foot of the stairs when he was letting me out; and I've always remembered the words and the tone as the first sign of the quickening drama of poor Brooksmith's fate. It was indeed an education, but to what was this sensitive young man of thirty-five, of the servile class, being educated?

Practically and inevitably, for the time, to companionship, to the perpetual, the even exaggerated reference and appeal of a person brought to dependence by his time of life and his infirmities and always addicted moreover—this was the exaggeration—to the art of giving you pleasure by letting you do things for him. There were certain things Mr. Offord was capable of pretending he liked you to do even when he didn't—this, I mean, if he thought *you* liked them. If it happened that you didn't either—which was rare, yet might be—of course there were cross-purposes; but Brooksmith was there to prevent their going very far. This was precisely the way he acted as moderator; he averted misunderstandings or cleared them up. He had been capable, strange as it may appear, of acquiring for this purpose an insight into the French tongue, which was often used at Mr. Offord's; for besides being habitual to most of the foreigners, and they were many, who haunted the place or arrived with letters—letters often requiring a little worried consideration, of which Brooksmith always had cognisance—it had really become the primary language of the master of the house. I don't know if all the malentendus were in French, but almost all the explanations were, and this didn't a bit prevent Brooksmith's following them. I know Mr. Offord used to read passages to him from Montaigne and Saint-Simon, for he read perpetually when alone—when *they* were alone, that is—and Brooksmith was always about. Perhaps you'll say no wonder Mr. Offord's butler regarded him as "rather mad." However, if I'm not sure what he thought about Montaigne I'm convinced he admired Saint-Simon. A certain feeling for letters must have rubbed off on him from the mere handling of his master's books, which he was always carrying to and fro and putting back in their places.

I often noticed that if an anecdote or a quotation, much more a lively discussion, was going forward, he would, if busy with the fire or the curtains, the lamp or the tea, find a pretext for remaining in the room till the point should be reached. If his purpose was to catch it you weren't discreet, you were in fact scarce human, to call him off, and I shall never forget a look, a hard stony stare—I caught it in its passage—which, one day when there were a good many people in the room, he fastened upon the footman who was helping him in the service and who, in an undertone, had asked him some irrelevant question. It was the only manifestation of harshness I ever observed on Brooksmith's part, and I at first wondered what was the matter. Then I became conscious that Mr. Offord was relating a very curious anecdote, never before perhaps made so public, and imparted to the narrator by an eye-witness of the fact, bearing on Lord Byron's life in Italy. Nothing would induce me to reproduce it here, but Brooksmith had been in danger of losing it. If I ever should venture to reproduce it I shall feel how much I lose in not having my fellow auditor to refer to.

The first day Mr Offord's door was closed was therefore a dark date in contemporary history. It was raining hard and my umbrella was wet, but Brooksmith received it from me exactly as if this were a preliminary for going upstairs. I observed however that instead of putting it away he held it poised and trickling over the rug, and I then became aware that he was looking at me with deep acknowledging eyes—his air of universal responsibility. I immediately understood—there was scarce need of question and answer as they passed between us. When I took in that our good friend had given up as never before, though only for the occasion, I exclaimed dolefully: "What a difference it will make—and to how many people!"

"I shall be one of them, sir!" said Brooksmith; and that was the beginning of the end.

Mr. Offord came down again, but the spell was broken, the great sign being that the conversation was for the first time not directed. It wandered and stumbled, a little frightened, like a lost child—it had let go the nurse's hand. "The worst of it is that now we shall talk about my health—*c'est la fin de tout*," Mr. Offord said when he reappeared; and then I recognised what a note of change that would be—for he had never tolerated anything so provincial. We "ran" to each other's health as little as to the daily weather.

The talk became ours, in a word—not his; and as ours, even when HE talked, it could only be inferior. In this form it was a distress to Brooksmith, whose attention now wandered from it altogether: he had so much closer a vision of his master's intimate conditions than our superficialities represented. There were better hours, and he was more in and out of the room, but I could see he was conscious of the decline, almost of the collapse, of our great institution. He seemed to wish to take counsel with me about it, to feel responsible for its going on in some form or other. When for the second period—the first had lasted several days—he had to tell me that his employer didn't receive, I half expected to hear him say after a moment "Do you think I ought to, sir, in his place?"—as he might have asked me, with the return of autumn, if I thought he had better light the drawing-room fire.

He had a resigned philosophic sense of what his guests—our guests, as I came to regard them in our colloquies—would expect. His feeling was that he wouldn't absolutely have approved of himself as a substitute for Mr. Offord; but he was so saturated with the religion of habit that he would have made, for our friends, the necessary sacrifice to the divinity. He would take them on a little further, till they could look about them. I think I saw him also mentally confronted with the opportunity to deal—for once in his life—with some of his own dumb preferences, his limitations of sympathy, *weeding* a little in prospect and returning to a purer tradition. It was not unknown to me that he considered that toward the end of our host's career a certain laxity of selection had crept in.

At last it came to be the case that we all found the closed door more often than the open one; but even when it was closed Brooksmith managed a crack for me to squeeze through; so that practically I never turned away without having paid a visit. The difference simply came to be that the visit was to Brooksmith. It took place in the hall, at the familiar foot of the stairs, and we didn't sit down, at least Brooksmith didn't; moreover it was devoted wholly to one topic and always had the air of being already over—beginning, so to say, at the end. But it was always interesting—it always gave me something to think about. It's true that the subject of my meditation was ever the same—ever "It's all very well, but what *will* become of Brooksmith?" Even my private answer to this question left me still unsatisfied. No doubt Mr. Offord would provide for him, but *what* would he provide?—that was the great point. He couldn't provide society; and society had become a necessity of Brooksmith's nature. I must add that he never showed a symptom of what I may call sordid solicitude—anxiety on his own account. He was rather livid and intensely grave, as befitted a man before whose eyes the "shade of that which once was great" was passing away. He had the solemnity of a person winding up, under depressing circumstances, a long-established and celebrated business; he was a kind of social executor or liquidator. But his manner seemed to testify exclusively to the uncertainty of *our* future. I couldn't in those days have afforded it—I lived in two rooms in Jermyn Street and didn't "keep a man"; but even if my income had permitted I shouldn't have ventured to say to Brooksmith (emulating Mr. Offord) "My dear fellow, I'll take you on." The whole tone of our intercourse was so much more an implication that it was I who should now want a lift. Indeed there was a tacit assurance in Brooksmith's whole attitude that he should have me on his mind.

One of the most assiduous members of our circle had been Lady Kenyon, and I remember his telling me one day that her ladyship had in spite of her own infirmities, lately much aggravated, been in person to inquire. In answer to this I remarked that she would feel it more than any one. Brooksmith had a pause before saying in a certain tone—there's no reproducing some of his tones—"I'll go and see her." I went to see her myself and learned he had waited on her; but when I said to her, in the form of a joke but with a core of earnest, that when all was over some of us ought to combine, to club together, and set Brooksmith up on his own account, she replied a trifle disappointingly: "Do you mean in a public-house?" I looked at her in a way that I think Brooksmith himself would have approved, and then I answered: "Yes, the Offord Arms." What I had meant of course was that for the love of art itself we ought to look to it that such a peculiar faculty and so much acquired experience shouldn't be wasted. I really think that if we had caused a few black-edged cards to be struck off and circulated—"Mr. Brooksmith will continue to receive on the old premises from four to seven; business carried on as usual during the alterations"—the greater number of us would have rallied.

Several times he took me upstairs—always by his own proposal—and our dear old friend, in bed (in a curious flowered and brocaded casaque which made him, especially as his head was tied up in a handkerchief to match, look, to my imagination, like the dying Voltaire) held for ten minutes a sadly shrunken little salon. I felt indeed each time as if I were attending the last coucher of some social sovereign. He was royally whimsical about his sufferings and not at all concerned—quite as if the Constitution provided for the case about his successor. He glided over *our* sufferings charmingly, and none of his jokes—it was a gallant abstention, some of them would have been so easy—were at our expense. Now and again, I confess, there was one at Brooksmith's, but so pathetically sociable as to make the excellent man look at me in a way that seemed to say: "Do exchange a glance with me, or I shan't be able to stand it." What he wasn't able to stand was not what Mr. Offord said about him, but what he wasn't able to say in return. His idea of conversation for himself was giving you the convenience of speaking to him; and when he went to "see" Lady Kenyon for instance it was to carry her the tribute of his receptive silence. Where would the speech of his betters have been if proper service had been a manifestation of sound? In that case the fundamental difference would have had to be shown by their dumbness, and many of them, poor things, were dumb enough without that provision. Brooksmith took an unfailing interest in the preservation of the fundamental difference; it was the thing he had most on his conscience.

What had become of it however when Mr. Offord passed away like any inferior person—was relegated to eternal stillness after the manner of a butler above-stairs? His aspect on the event—for the several successive days—may be imagined, and the multiplication by funereal observance of the things he didn't say. When everything was over—it was late the same day—I knocked at the door of the house of mourning as I so often had done before. I could never call on Mr. Offord again, but I had come literally to call on Brooksmith. I wanted to ask him if there was anything I could do for him, tainted with vagueness as this inquiry could only be. My presumptuous dream of taking him into my own service had died away: my service wasn't worth his being taken into. My offer could only be to help him to find another place, and yet there was an indelicacy, as it were, in taking for granted that his thoughts would immediately be fixed on another. I had a hope that he would be able to give his life a different form—though certainly not the form, the frequent result of such bereavements, of his setting up a little shop. That would have been dreadful; for I should have wished to forward any enterprise he might embark in, yet how could I have brought myself to go and pay him shillings and take back coppers, over a counter? My visit then was simply an intended compliment. He took it as such, gratefully and with all the tact in the world. He knew I really couldn't help him and that I knew he knew I couldn't; but we discussed the situation—with a good deal of elegant generality—at the foot of the stairs, in the hall already dismantled, where I had so often discussed other situations with him. The executors were in possession, as was still more apparent when he made me pass for a few minutes into the dining-room, where various objects were muffled up for removal.

Two definite facts, however, he had to communicate; one being that he was to leave the house for ever that night (servants, for some mysterious reason, seem always to depart by night), and the other—he mentioned it only at the last and with hesitation—that he was already aware his late master had left him a legacy of eighty pounds. "I'm very glad," I said, and Brooksmith was of the same mind: "It was so like him to think of me." This was all that passed between us on the subject, and I know nothing of his judgement of Mr. Offord's memento. Eighty pounds are always eighty pounds, and no one has ever left ME an equal sum; but, all the same, for Brooksmith, I was disappointed. I don't know what I had expected, but it was almost a shock. Eighty pounds might stock a small shop—a *very* small shop; but, I repeat, I couldn't bear to think of that. I asked my friend if he had been able to save a little, and he replied: "No, sir; I've had to do things." I didn't inquire what things they might have been; they were his own affair, and I took his word for them as assentingly as if he had had the greatness of an ancient house to keep up; especially as there was something in his manner that seemed to convey a prospect of further sacrifice.

"I shall have to turn round a bit, sir—I shall have to look about me," he said; and then he added indulgently, magnanimously: "If you should happen to hear of anything for me—"

I couldn't let him finish; this was, in its essence, too much in the really grand manner. It would be a help to my getting him off my mind to be able to pretend I *could* find the right place, and that help he wished to give me, for it was doubtless painful to him to see me in so false a position. I interposed with a few words to the effect of how well aware I was that wherever he should go, whatever he should do, he would miss our old friend terribly—miss him even more than I should, having been with him so much more. This led him to make the speech that has remained with me as the very text of the whole episode.

"Oh sir, it's sad for *you*, very sad indeed, and for a great many gentlemen and ladies; that it is, sir. But for me, sir, it is, if I may say so, still graver even than that: it's just the loss of something that was everything. For me, sir," he went on with rising tears, "he was just *all*, if you know what I mean, sir. You have others, sir, I daresay—not that I would have you understand me to speak of them as in any way tantamount. But you have the pleasures of society, sir; if it's only in talking about him, sir, as I daresay you do freely—for all his blest memory has to fear from it—with gentlemen and ladies who have had the same honour. That's not for me, sir, and I've to keep my associations to myself. Mr. Offord was MY society, and now, you see, I just haven't any. You go back to conversation, sir, after all, and I go back to my place," Brooksmith stammered, without exaggerated irony or dramatic bitterness, but with a flat unstudied veracity and his hand on the knob of the street-door. He turned it to let me out and then he added: "I just go downstairs, sir, again, and I stay there."

"My poor child," I replied in my emotion, quite as Mr. Offord used to speak, "my dear fellow, leave it to me: WE'LL look after you, we'll all do something for you."

"Ah if you could give me some one *like* him! But there ain't two such in the world," Brooksmith said as we parted.

He had given me his address—the place where he would be to be heard of. For a long time I had no occasion to make use of the information: he proved on trial so very difficult a case. The people who knew him and had known Mr. Offord didn't want to take him, and yet I couldn't bear to try to thrust him among strangers—strangers to his past when not to his present. I spoke to many of our old friends about him and found them all governed by the odd mixture of feelings of which I myself was conscious—as well as disposed, further, to entertain a suspicion that he was "spoiled," with which, I then would have nothing to do. In plain terms a certain embarrassment, a sensible awkwardness when they thought of it, attached to the idea of using him as a menial: they had met him so often in society. Many of them would have asked him, and did ask him, or rather did ask me to ask him, to come and see them, but a mere visiting-list was not what I wanted for him. He was too short for people who were very particular; nevertheless I heard of an opening in a diplomatic household which led me to write him a note, though I was looking much less for something grand than for something human. Five days later I heard from him. The secretary's wife had decided, after keeping him waiting till then, that she couldn't take a servant out of a house in which there hadn't been a lady. The note had a P.S.: "It's a good job there wasn't, sir, such a lady as some."

A week later he came to see me and told me he was "suited," committed to some highly respectable people—they were something quite immense in the City—who lived on the Bayswater side of the Park. "I daresay it will be rather poor, sir," he admitted; "but I've seen the fireworks, haven't I, sir?—it can't be fireworks *every* night. After Mansfield Street there ain't much choice." There was a certain amount, however, it seemed; for the following year, calling one day on a country cousin, a lady of a certain age who was spending a fortnight in town with some friends of her own, a family unknown to me and resident in Chester Square, the door of the house was opened, to my surprise and gratification, by Brooksmith in person. When I came out I had some conversation with him from which I gathered that he had found the large City people too dull for endurance, and I guessed, though he didn't say it, that he had found them vulgar as well. I don't know what judgement he would have passed on his actual patrons if my relative hadn't been their friend; but in view of that connexion he abstained from comment.

None was necessary, however, for before the lady in question brought her visit to a close they honoured me with an invitation to dinner, which I accepted. There was a largeish party on the occasion, but I confess I thought of Brooksmith rather more than of the seated company. They required no depth of attention—they were all referable to usual irredeemable inevitable types. It was the world of cheerful commonplace and conscious gentility and prosperous density, a full-fed material insular world, a world of hideous florid plate and ponderous order and thin conversation. There wasn't a word said about Byron, or even about a minor bard then much in view. Nothing would have induced me to look at Brooksmith in the course of the repast, and I felt sure that not even my overturning the wine would have induced him to meet my eye. We were in intellectual sympathy—we felt, as regards each other, a degree of social responsibility. In short we had been in Arcadia together, and we had both come to *this*! No wonder we were ashamed to be confronted. When he had helped on my overcoat, as I was going away, we parted, for the first time since the earliest days of Mansfield Street, in silence. I thought he looked lean and wasted, and I guessed that his new place wasn't more "human" than his previous one. There was plenty of beef and beer, but there was no reciprocity. The question for him to have asked before accepting the position wouldn't have been "How many footmen are kept?" but "How much imagination?"

The next time I went to the house—I confess it wasn't very soon—I encountered his successor, a personage who evidently enjoyed the good fortune of never having quitted his natural level. Could any be higher? he seemed to ask—over the heads of three footmen and even of some visitors. He made me feel as if Brooksmith were dead; but I didn't dare to inquire—I couldn't have borne his "I haven't the least idea, sir." I despatched a note to the address that worthy had given me after Mr. Offord's death, but I received no answer. Six months later however I was favoured with a visit from an elderly dreary dingy person who introduced herself to me as Mr. Brooksmith's aunt and from whom I learned that he was out of place and out of health and had allowed her to come and say to me that if I could spare half an hour to look in at him he would take it as a rare honour.

I went the next day—his messenger had given me a new address—and found my friend lodged in a short sordid street in Marylebone, one of those corners of London that wear the last expression of sickly meanness. The room into which I was shown was above the small establishment of a dyer and cleaner who had inflated kid gloves and discoloured shawls in his shop-front. There was a great deal of grimy infant life up and down the place, and there was a hot moist smell within, as of the "boiling" of dirty linen. Brooksmith sat with a blanket over his legs at a clean little window where, from behind stiff bluish-white curtains, he could look across at a huckster's and a tinsmith's and a small greasy public-house. He had passed through an illness and was convalescent, and his mother, as well as his aunt, was in attendance on him. I liked the nearer relative, who was bland and intensely humble, but I had my doubts of the remoter, whom I connected perhaps unjustly with the opposite public-house—she seemed somehow greasy with the same grease—and whose furtive eye followed every movement of my hand as to see if it weren't going into my pocket. It didn't take this direction—I couldn't, unsolicited, put myself at that sort of ease with Brooksmith. Several times the door of the room opened and mysterious old women peeped in and shuffled back again. I don't know who they were; poor Brooksmith seemed encompassed with vague prying beery females.

He was vague himself, and evidently weak, and much embarrassed, and not an allusion was made between us to Mansfield Street. The vision of the salon of which he had been an ornament hovered before me however, by contrast, sufficiently. He assured me he was really getting better, and his mother remarked that he would come round if he could only get his spirits up. The aunt echoed this opinion, and I became more sure that in her own case she knew where to go for such a purpose. I'm afraid I was rather weak with my old friend, for I neglected the opportunity, so exceptionally good, to rebuke the levity which had led him to throw up honourable positions—fine stiff steady berths in Bayswater and Belgravia, with morning prayers, as I knew, attached to one of them. Very likely his reasons had been profane and sentimental; he didn't want morning prayers, he wanted to be somebody's dear fellow; but I couldn't be the person to rebuke him. He shuffled these episodes out of sight—I saw he had no wish to discuss them. I noted further, strangely enough, that it would probably be a questionable pleasure for him to see me again: he doubted now even of my power to condone his aberrations. He didn't wish to have to explain; and his behaviour was likely in future to need explanation. When I bade him farewell he looked at me a moment with eyes that said everything: "How can I talk about those exquisite years in this place, before these people, with the old women poking their heads in? It was very good of you to come to see me; it wasn't my idea—*she* brought you. We've said everything; it's over; you'll lose all patience with me, and I'd rather you shouldn't see the rest." I sent him some money in a letter the next day, but I saw the rest only in the light of a barren sequel.

A whole year after my visit to him I became aware once, in dining out, that Brooksmith was one of the several servants who hovered behind our chairs. He hadn't opened the door of the house to me, nor had I recognised him in the array of retainers in the hall. This time I tried to catch his eye, but he never gave me a chance, and when he handed me a dish I could only be careful to thank him audibly. Indeed I partook of two *entrées* of which I had my doubts, subsequently converted into certainties, in order not to snub him. He looked well enough in health, but much older, and wore in an exceptionally marked degree the glazed and expressionless mask of the British domestic *de race*. I saw with dismay that if I hadn't known him I should have taken him, on the showing of his countenance, for an extravagant illustration of irresponsive servile gloom. I said to myself that he had become a reactionary, gone over to the Philistines, thrown himself into religion, the religion of his "place," like a foreign lady *sur le retour*. I divined moreover that he was only engaged for the evening—he had become a mere waiter, had joined the band of the white-waistcoated who "go out." There was something pathetic in this fact—it was a terrible vulgarisation of Brooksmith. It was the mercenary prose of butlerhood; he had given up the struggle for the poetry. If reciprocity was what he had missed where was the reciprocity now? Only in the bottoms of the wine-glasses and the five shillings—or whatever they get— clapped into his hand by the permanent man. However, I supposed he had taken up a precarious branch of his profession because it after all sent him less downstairs. His relations with London society were more superficial, but they were of course more various. As I went away on this occasion I looked out for him eagerly among the four or five attendants whose perpendicular persons, fluting the walls of London passages, are supposed to lubricate the process of departure; but he was not on duty. I asked one of the others if he were not in the house, and received the prompt answer: "Just left, sir. Anything I can do for you, sir?" I wanted to say "Please give him my kind regards"; but I abstained—I didn't want to compromise him; and I never came across him again.

Often and often, in dining out, I looked for him, sometimes accepting invitations on purpose to multiply the chances of my meeting him. But always in vain; so that as I met many other members of the casual class over and over again I at last adopted the theory that he always procured a list of expected guests beforehand and kept away from the banquets which he thus learned I was to grace. At last I gave up hope, and one day at the end of three years I received another visit from his aunt. She was drearier and dingier, almost squalid, and she was in great tribulation and want. Her sister, Mrs. Brooksmith, had been dead a year, and three months later her nephew had disappeared. He had always looked after her a bit since her troubles; I never knew what her troubles had been—and now she hadn't so much as a petticoat to pawn. She had also a niece, to whom she had been everything before her troubles, but the niece had treated her most shameful. These were details; the great and romantic fact was Brooksmith's final evasion of his fate. He had gone out to wait one evening as usual, in a white waistcoat she had done up for him with her own hands—being due at a large party up Kensington way. But he had never come home again and had never arrived at the large party, nor at any party that any one could make out. No trace of him had come to light—no gleam of the white waistcoat had pierced the obscurity of his doom. This news was a sharp shock to me, for I had my ideas about his real destination. His aged relative had promptly, as she said, guessed the worst. Somehow, and somewhere he had got out of the way altogether, and now I trust that, with characteristic deliberation, he is changing the plates of the immortal gods. As my depressing visitant also said, he never *had* got his spirits up. I was fortunately able to dismiss her with her own somewhat improved. But the dim ghost of poor Brooksmith is one of those that I see. He had indeed been spoiled.

THE REAL THING

CHAPTER I

When the porter's wife, who used to answer the house-bell, announced "A gentleman and a lady, sir," I had, as I often had in those days—the wish being father to the thought—an immediate vision of sitters. Sitters my visitors in this case proved to be; but not in the sense I should have preferred. There was nothing at first however to indicate that they mightn't have come for a portrait. The gentleman, a man of fifty, very high and very straight, with a moustache slightly grizzled and a dark grey walking-coat admirably fitted, both of which I noted professionally—I don't mean as a barber or yet as a tailor—would have struck me as a celebrity if celebrities often were striking. It was a truth of which I had for some time been conscious that a figure with a good deal of frontage was, as one might say, almost never a public institution. A glance at the lady helped to remind me of this paradoxical law: she also looked too distinguished to be a "personality." Moreover one would scarcely come across two variations together.

Neither of the pair immediately spoke—they only prolonged the preliminary gaze suggesting that each wished to give the other a chance. They were visibly shy; they stood there letting me take them in—which, as I afterwards perceived, was the most practical thing they could have done. In this way their embarrassment served their cause. I had seen people painfully reluctant to mention that they desired anything so gross as to be represented on canvas; but the scruples of my new friends appeared almost insurmountable. Yet the gentleman might have said "I should like a portrait of my wife," and the lady might have said "I should like a portrait of my husband." Perhaps they weren't husband and wife—this naturally would make the matter more delicate. Perhaps they wished to be done together—in which case they ought to have brought a third person to break the news.

"We come from Mr. Rivet," the lady finally said with a dim smile that had the effect of a moist sponge passed over a "sunk" piece of painting, as well as of a vague allusion to vanished beauty. She was as tall and straight, in her degree, as her companion, and with ten years less to carry. She looked as sad as a woman could look whose face was not charged with expression; that is her tinted oval mask showed waste as an exposed surface shows friction. The hand of time had played over her freely, but to an effect of elimination. She was slim and stiff, and so well-dressed, in dark blue cloth, with lappets and pockets and buttons, that it was clear she employed the same tailor as her husband. The couple had an indefinable air of prosperous thrift—they evidently got a good deal of luxury for their money. If I was to be one of their luxuries it would behove me to consider my terms.

"Ah Claude Rivet recommended me?" I echoed and I added that it was very kind of him, though I could reflect that, as he only painted landscape, this wasn't a sacrifice.

The lady looked very hard at the gentleman, and the gentleman looked round the room. Then staring at the floor a moment and stroking his moustache, he rested his pleasant eyes on me with the remark: "He said you were the right one."

"I try to be, when people want to sit."

"Yes, we should like to," said the lady anxiously.

"Do you mean together?"

My visitors exchanged a glance. "If you could do anything with ME I suppose it would be double," the gentleman stammered.

"Oh yes, there's naturally a higher charge for two figures than for one."

"We should like to make it pay," the husband confessed.

"That's very good of you," I returned, appreciating so unwonted a sympathy—for I supposed he meant pay the artist.

A sense of strangeness seemed to dawn on the lady. "We mean for the illustrations—Mr. Rivet said you might put one in."

"Put in—an illustration?" I was equally confused.

"Sketch her off, you know," said the gentleman, colouring.

It was only then that I understood the service Claude Rivet had rendered me; he had told them how I worked in black-and-white, for magazines, for story-books, for sketches of contemporary life, and consequently had copious employment for models. These things were true, but it was not less true—I may confess it now; whether because the aspiration was to lead to everything or to nothing I leave the reader to guess—that I couldn't get the honours, to say nothing of the emoluments, of a great painter of portraits out of my head. My "illustrations" were my pot-boilers; I looked to a different branch of art— far and away the most interesting it had always seemed to me—to perpetuate my fame. There was no shame in looking to it also to make my fortune but that fortune was by so much further from being made from the moment my visitors wished to be "done" for nothing. I was disappointed; for in the pictorial sense I had immediately *seen* them. I had seized their type—I had already settled what I would do with it. Something that wouldn't absolutely have pleased them, I afterwards reflected.

"Ah you're—you're—a—?" I began as soon as I had mastered my surprise. I couldn't bring out the dingy word "models": it seemed so little to fit the case.

"We haven't had much practice," said the lady.

"We've got to do something, and we've thought that an artist in your line might perhaps make something of us," her husband threw off. He further mentioned that they didn't know many artists and that they had gone first, on the off-chance—he painted views of course, but sometimes put in figures; perhaps I remembered—to Mr. Rivet, whom they had met a few years before at a place in Norfolk where he was sketching.

"We used to sketch a little ourselves," the lady hinted.

"It's very awkward, but we absolutely must do something," her husband went on.

31

"Of course we're not so *very* young," she admitted with a wan smile.

With the remark that I might as well know something more about them the husband had handed me a card extracted from a neat new pocket-book—their appurtenances were all of the freshest—and inscribed with the words "Major Monarch." Impressive as these words were they didn't carry my knowledge much further; but my visitor presently added: "I've left the army and we've had the misfortune to lose our money. In fact our means are dreadfully small."

"It's awfully trying—a regular strain,", said Mrs. Monarch.

They evidently wished to be discreet—to take care not to swagger because they were gentlefolk. I felt them willing to recognise this as something of a drawback, at the same time that I guessed at an underlying sense—their consolation in adversity—that they *had* their points. They certainly had; but these advantages struck me as preponderantly social; such for instance as would help to make a drawing-room look well. However, a drawing-room was always, or ought to be, a picture.

In consequence of his wife's allusion to their age Major Monarch observed: "Naturally it's more for the figure that we thought of going in. We can still hold ourselves up." On the instant I saw that the figure was indeed their strong point. His "naturally" didn't sound vain, but it lighted up the question. "*She* has the best one," he continued, nodding at his wife with a pleasant after-dinner absence of circumlocution. I could only reply, as if we were in fact sitting over our wine, that this didn't prevent his own from being very good; which led him in turn to make answer: "We thought that if you ever have to do people like us we might be something like it. *She* particularly—for a lady in a book, you know."

I was so amused by them that, to get more of it, I did my best to take their point of view; and though it was an embarrassment to find myself appraising physically, as if they were animals on hire or useful blacks, a pair whom I should have expected to meet only in one of the relations in which criticism is tacit, I looked at Mrs. Monarch judicially enough to be able to exclaim after a moment with conviction: "Oh yes, a lady in a book!" She was singularly like a bad illustration.

"We'll stand up, if you like," said the Major; and he raised himself before me with a really grand air.

I could take his measure at a glance—he was six feet two and a perfect gentleman. It would have paid any club in process of formation and in want of a stamp to engage him at a salary to stand in the principal window. What struck me at once was that in coming to me they had rather missed their vocation; they could surely have been turned to better account for advertising purposes. I couldn't of course see the thing in detail, but I could see them make somebody's fortune—I don't mean their own. There was something in them for a waistcoat-maker, an hotel-keeper or a soap-vendor. I could imagine "We always use it" pinned on their bosoms with the greatest effect; I had a vision of the brilliancy with which they would launch a table d'hôte.

Mrs. Monarch sat still, not from pride but from shyness, and presently her husband said to her: "Get up, my dear, and show how smart you are." She obeyed, but she had no need to get up to show it. She walked to the end of the studio and then came back blushing, her fluttered eyes on the partner of her appeal. I was reminded of an incident I had accidentally had a glimpse of in Paris—being with a friend there, a dramatist about to produce a play, when an actress came to him to ask to be entrusted with a part. She went through her paces before him, walked up and down as Mrs. Monarch was doing. Mrs. Monarch did it quite as well, but I abstained from applauding. It was very odd to see such people apply for such poor pay. She looked as if she had ten thousand a year. Her husband had used the word that described her: she was in the London current jargon essentially and typically "smart." Her figure was, in the same order of ideas, conspicuously and irreproachably "good." For a woman of her age her waist was surprisingly small; her elbow moreover had the orthodox crook. She held her head at the conventional angle, but why did she come to ME? She ought to have tried on jackets at a big shop. I feared my visitors were not only destitute but "artistic"—which would be a great complication. When she sat down again I thanked her, observing that what a draughtsman most valued in his model was the faculty of keeping quiet.

"Oh *she* can keep quiet," said Major Monarch. Then he added jocosely: "I've always kept her quiet."

"I'm not a nasty fidget, am I?" It was going to wring tears from me, I felt, the way she hid her head, ostrich-like, in the other broad bosom.

The owner of this expanse addressed his answer to me. "Perhaps it isn't out of place to mention—because we ought to be quite business-like, oughtn't we?—that when I married her she was known as the Beautiful Statue."

"Oh dear!" said Mrs. Monarch ruefully.

"Of course I should want a certain amount of expression," I rejoined.

"Of *course*!"—and I had never heard such unanimity.

"And then I suppose you know that you'll get awfully tired."

"Oh we *never* get tired!" they eagerly cried.

"Have you had any kind of practice?"

They hesitated—they looked at each other. "We've been photographed—*immensely*," said Mrs. Monarch.

"She means the fellows have asked us themselves," added the Major.

"I see—because you're so good-looking."

"I don't know what they thought, but they were always after us."

"We always got our photographs for nothing," smiled Mrs. Monarch.

"We might have brought some, my dear," her husband remarked.

"I'm not sure we have any left. We've given quantities away," she explained to me.

"With our autographs and that sort of thing," said the Major.

"Are they to be got in the shops?" I inquired as a harmless pleasantry.

"Oh yes, *hers*—they used to be."

"Not now," said Mrs. Monarch with her eyes on the floor.

CHAPTER II

I could fancy the "sort of thing" they put on the presentation copies of their photographs, and I was sure they wrote a beautiful hand. It was odd how quickly I was sure of everything that concerned them. If they were now so poor as to have to cam shillings and pence they could never have had much of a margin. Their good looks had been their capital, and they had good-humouredly made the most of the career that this resource marked out for them. It was in their faces, the blankness, the deep intellectual repose of the twenty years of country-house visiting that had given them pleasant intonations. I could see the sunny drawing-rooms, sprinkled with periodicals she didn't read, in which Mrs. Monarch had continuously sat; I could see the wet shrubberies in which she had walked, equipped to admiration for either exercise. I could see the rich covers the Major had helped to shoot and the wonderful garments in which, late at night, he repaired to the smoking-room to talk about them. I could imagine their leggings and waterproofs, their knowing tweeds and rugs, their rolls of sticks and cases of tackle and neat umbrellas; and I could evoke the exact appearance of their servants and the compact variety of their luggage on the platforms of country stations.

They gave small tips, but they were liked; they didn't do anything themselves, but they were welcome. They looked so well everywhere; they gratified the general relish for stature, complexion and "form." They knew it without fatuity or vulgarity, and they respected themselves in consequence. They weren't superficial: they were thorough and kept themselves up—it had been their line. People with such a taste for activity had to have some line. I could feel how even in a dull house they could have been counted on for the joy of life. At present something had happened—it didn't matter what, their little income had grown less, it had grown least—and they had to do something for pocket-money. Their friends could like them, I made out, without liking to support them. There was something about them that represented credit— their clothes, their manners, their type; but if credit is a large empty pocket in which an occasional chink reverberates, the chink at least must be audible.

What they wanted of me was help to make it so. Fortunately they had no children—I soon divined that. They would also perhaps wish our relations to be kept secret: this was why it was "for the figure"—the reproduction of the face would betray them.

I liked them—I felt, quite as their friends must have done—they were so simple; and I had no objection to them if they would suit. But somehow with all their perfections I didn't easily believe in them. After all they were amateurs, and the ruling passion of my life was—the detestation of the amateur. Combined with this was another perversity—an innate preference for the represented subject over the real one: the defect of the real one was so apt to be a lack of representation. I liked things that appeared; then one was sure. Whether they *were* or not was a subordinate and almost always a profitless question. There were other considerations, the first of which was that I already had two or three recruits in use, notably a young person with big feet, in alpaca, from Kilburn, who for a couple of years had come to me regularly for my illustrations and with whom I was still—perhaps ignobly—satisfied. I frankly explained to my visitors how the case stood, but they had taken more precautions than I supposed. They had reasoned out their opportunity, for Claude Rivet had told them of the projected *édition de luxe* of one of the writers of our day—the rarest of the novelists—who, long neglected by the multitudinous vulgar, and dearly prized by the attentive (need I mention Philip Vincent?) had had the happy fortune of seeing, late in life, the dawn and then the full light of a higher criticism; an estimate in which on the part of the public there was something really of expiation. The edition preparing, planned by a publisher of taste, was practically an act of high reparation; the woodcuts with which it was to be enriched were the homage of English art to one of the most independent representatives of English letters. Major and Mrs. Monarch confessed to me they had hoped I might be able to work *them* into my branch of the enterprise. They knew I was to do the first of the books, Rutland Ramsay, but I had to make clear to them that my participation in the rest of the affair—this first book was to be a test—must depend on the satisfaction I should give. If this should be limited my employers would drop me with scarce common forms. It was therefore a crisis for me, and naturally I was making special preparations, looking about for new people, should they be necessary, and securing the best types. I admitted however that I should like to settle down to two or three good models who would do for everything.

"Should we have often to—a—put on special clothes?" Mrs. Monarch timidly demanded.

"Dear yes—that's half the business."

"And should we be expected to supply our own costumes?

"Oh no; I've got a lot of things. A painter's models put on—or put off—anything he likes."

"And you mean—a—the same?"

"The same?"

Mrs. Monarch looked at her husband again.

"Oh she was just wondering," he explained, "if the costumes are in *general* use." I had to confess that they were, and I mentioned further that some of them—I had a lot of, genuine greasy last-century things—had served their time, a hundred years ago, on living, world-stained men and women; on figures not perhaps so far removed, in that vanished world, from *their* type, the Monarchs', *quoi*! of a breeched and bewigged age. "We'll put, on anything that *fits*," said the Major.

"Oh I arrange that—they fit in the pictures."

"I'm afraid I should do better for the modern books. I'd come as you like," said Mrs. Monarch.

"She has got a lot of clothes at home: they might do for contemporary life," her husband continued.

"Oh I can fancy scenes in which you'd be quite natural." And indeed I could see the slipshod re-arrangements of stale properties—the stories I tried to produce pictures for without the exasperation of reading them—whose sandy tracts the good lady might help to people. But I had to return to the fact that—for this sort of work—the daily mechanical grind—I was already equipped: the people I was working with were fully adequate.

"We only thought we might be more like *some* characters," said Mrs. Monarch mildly, getting up.

Her husband also rose; he stood looking at me with a dim wistfulness that was touching in so fine a man. "Wouldn't it be rather a pull sometimes to have—a—to have—?" He hung fire; he wanted me to help him by phrasing what he meant. But I couldn't—I didn't know. So he brought it out awkwardly: "The *real* thing; a gentleman, you know, or a lady." I was quite ready to give a general assent—I admitted that there was a great deal in that. This encouraged Major Monarch to say, following up his appeal with an unacted gulp: "It's awfully hard—we've tried everything." The gulp was communicative; it proved too much for his wife. Before I knew it Mrs. Monarch had dropped again upon a divan and burst into tears. Her husband sat down beside her, holding one of her hands; whereupon she quickly dried her eyes with the other, while I felt embarrassed as she looked up at me. "There isn't a confounded job I haven't applied for—waited for—prayed for. You can fancy we'd be pretty bad first. Secretaryships and that sort of thing? You might as well ask for a peerage. I'd be *anything*—I'm strong; a messenger or a coalheaver. I'd put on a gold-laced cap and open carriage-doors in front of the haberdasher's; I'd hang about a station to carry portmanteaux; I'd be a postman. But they won't *look* at you; there are thousands as good as yourself already on the ground. *Gentlemen*, poor beggars, who've drunk their wine, who've kept their hunters!"

I was as reassuring as I knew how to be, and my visitors were presently on their feet again while, for the experiment, we agreed on an hour. We were discussing it when the door opened and Miss Churm came in with a wet umbrella. Miss Churm had to take the omnibus to Maida Vale and then walk half a mile. She looked a trifle blowsy and slightly splashed. I scarcely ever saw her come in without thinking afresh how odd it was that, being so little in herself, she should yet be so much in others. She was a meagre little Miss Churm, but was such an ample heroine of romance. She was only a freckled cockney, but she could represent everything, from a fine lady to a shepherdess, she had the faculty as she might have had a fine voice or long hair. She couldn't spell and she loved beer, but she had two or three "points," and practice, and a knack, and mother-wit, and a whimsical sensibility, and a love of the theatre, and seven sisters,—and not an ounce of respect, especially for the H. The first thing my visitors saw was that her umbrella was wet, and in their spotless perfection they visibly winced at it. The rain had come on since their arrival.

"I'm all in a soak; there *was* a mess of people in the 'bus. I wish you lived near a stytion," said Miss Churm. I requested her to get ready as quickly as possible, and she passed into the room in which she always changed her dress. But before going out she asked me what she was to get into this time.

"It's the Russian princess, don't you know?" I answered; "the one with the 'golden eyes,' in black velvet, for the long thing in the *Cheapside*."

"Golden eyes? I *say!*" cried Miss Churm, while my companions watched her with intensity as she withdrew. She always arranged herself, when she was late, before I could turn round; and I kept my visitors a little on purpose, so that they might get an idea, from seeing her, what would be expected of themselves. I mentioned that she was quite my notion of an excellent model—she was really very clever.

"Do you think she looks like a Russian princess?" Major Monarch asked with lurking alarm.

"When I make her, yes."

"Oh if you have to *make* her—!" he reasoned, not without point.

"That's the most you can ask. There are so many who are not makeable."

"Well now, *here's* a lady"—and with a persuasive smile he passed his arm into his wife's—"who's already made!"

"Oh I'm not a Russian princess," Mrs. Monarch protested a little coldly. I could see she had known some and didn't like them. There at once was a complication of a kind I never had to fear with Miss Churm.

This young lady came back in black velvet—the gown was rather rusty and very low on her lean shoulders—and with a Japanese fan in her red hands. I reminded her that in the scene I was doing she had to look over some one's head. "I forget whose it is but it doesn't matter. Just look over a head."

"I'd rather look over a stove," said Miss Churm and she took her station near the fire. She fell into Position, settled herself into a tall attitude, gave a certain backward inclination to her head and a certain forward droop to her fan, and looked, at least to my prejudiced sense, distinguished and charming, foreign and dangerous. We left her looking so while I went downstairs with Major and Mrs. Monarch.

"I believe I could come about as near it as that," said Mrs. Monarch.

"Oh you think she's shabby, but you must allow for the alchemy of art."

However, they went off with an evident increase of comfort founded on their demonstrable advantage in being the real thing. I could fancy them shuddering over Miss Churm. She was very droll about them when I went back, for I told her what they wanted.

"Well, if *she* can sit I'll tyke to bookkeeping," said my model.

"She's very ladylike," I replied as an innocent form of aggravation.

"So much the worse for *you*. That means she can't turn round."

"She'll do for the fashionable novels."

"Oh yes, she'll DO for them!" my model humorously declared. "Ain't they bad enough without her?" I had often sociably denounced them to Miss Churm.

CHAPTER III

It was for the elucidation of a mystery in one of these works that I first tried Mrs. Monarch. Her husband came with her, to be useful if necessary—it was sufficiently clear that as a general thing he would prefer to come with her. At first I wondered if this were for "propriety's" sake—if he were going to be jealous and meddling. The idea was too tiresome, and if it had been confirmed it would speedily have brought our acquaintance to a close. But I soon saw there was nothing in it and that if he accompanied Mrs. Monarch it was—in addition to the chance of being wanted—simply because he had nothing else to do. When they were separate his occupation was gone, and they never *had* been separate. I judged rightly that in their awkward situation their close union was their main comfort and that this union had no weak spot. It was a real marriage, an encouragement to the hesitating, a nut for pessimists to crack. Their address was humble—I remember afterwards thinking it had been the only thing about them that was really professional—and I could fancy the lamentable lodgings in which the Major would have been left alone. He could sit there more or less grimly with his wife—he couldn't sit there anyhow without her.

He had too much tact to try and make himself agreeable when he couldn't be useful; so when I was too absorbed in my work to talk he simply sat and waited. But I liked to hear him talk—it made my work, when not interrupting it, less mechanical, less special. To listen to him was to combine the excitement of going out with the economy of staying at home. There was only one hindrance—that I seemed not to know any of the people this brilliant couple had known. I think he wondered extremely, during the term of our intercourse, whom the deuce I *did* know. He hadn't a stray sixpence of an idea to fumble for, so we didn't spin it very fine; we confined ourselves to questions of leather and even of liquor-saddlers and breeches-makers and how to get excellent claret cheap—and matters like "good trains" and the habits of small game. His lore on these last subjects was astonishing—he managed to interweave the station-master with the ornithologist. When he couldn't talk about greater things he could talk cheerfully about smaller, and since I couldn't accompany him into reminiscences of the fashionable world he could lower the conversation without a visible effort to my level.

So earnest a desire to please was touching in a man who could so easily have knocked one down. He looked after the fire and had an opinion on the draught of the stove without my asking him, and I could see that he thought many of my arrangements not half knowing. I remember telling him that if I were only rich I'd offer him a salary to come and teach me how to live. Sometimes he gave a random sigh of which the essence might have been: "Give me even such a bare old-barrack as this, and I'd do something with it!" When I wanted to use him he came alone; which was an illustration of the superior courage of women. His wife could bear her solitary second floor, and she was in general more discreet; showing by various small reserves that she was alive to the propriety of keeping our relations markedly professional— not letting them slide into sociability. She wished it to remain clear that she and the Major were employed, not cultivated, and if she approved of me as a superior, who could be kept in his place, she never thought me quite good enough for an equal.

She sat with great intensity, giving the whole of her mind to it, and was capable of remaining for an hour almost as motionless as before a photographer's lens. I could see she had been photographed often, but somehow the very habit that made her good for that purpose unfitted her for mine. At first I was extremely pleased with her ladylike air, and it was a satisfaction, on coming to follow her lines, to see how good they were and how far they could lead the pencil. But after a little skirmishing I began to find her too insurmountably stiff; do what I would with it my drawing looked like a photograph or a copy of a photograph. Her figure had no variety of expression—she herself had no sense of variety. You may say that this was my business and was only a question of placing her. Yet I placed her in every conceivable position and she managed to obliterate their differences. She was always a lady certainly, and into the bargain was always the same lady. She was the real thing, but always the same thing. There were moments when I rather writhed under the serenity of her confidence that she *was* the real thing. All her dealings with me and all her husband's were an implication that this was lucky for ME. Meanwhile I found myself trying to invent types that approached her own, instead of making her own transform itself—in the clever way that was not impossible for instance to poor Miss Churm. Arrange as I would and take the precautions I would, she always came out, in my pictures, too tall—landing me in the dilemma of having represented a fascinating woman as seven feet high, which (out of respect perhaps to my own very much scantier inches) was far from my idea of such a personage.

The case was worse with the Major—nothing I could do would keep *him* down, so that he became useful only for the representation of brawny giants. I adored variety and range, I cherished human accidents, the illustrative note; I wanted to characterise closely, and the thing in the world I most hated was the danger of being ridden by a type. I had quarrelled with some of my friends about it; I had parted company with them for maintaining that one *had* to be, and that if the type was beautiful—witness Raphael and Leonardo—the servitude was only a gain. I was neither Leonardo nor Raphael—I might only be a presumptuous young modern searcher; but I held that everything was to be sacrificed sooner than character. When they claimed that the obsessional form could easily BE character I retorted, perhaps superficially, "Whose?" It couldn't be everybody's—it might end in being nobody's.

After I had drawn Mrs. Monarch a dozen times I felt surer even than before that the value of such a model as Miss Churm resided precisely in the fact that she had no positive stamp, combined of course with the other fact that what she did have was a curious and inexplicable talent for imitation. Her usual appearance was like a curtain which—she could draw up at request for a capital performance. This performance was simply suggestive; but it was a word to the wise—it was vivid and pretty. Sometimes even I thought it, though she was plain herself, too insipidly pretty; I made it a reproach to her that the figures drawn from her were monotonously (*bêtement*, as we used to say) graceful. Nothing made her more angry: it was so much her pride to feel she could sit for characters that had nothing in common with each other. She would accuse me at such moments of taking away her "reputytion."

It suffered a certain shrinkage, this queer quantity, from the repeated visits of my new friends. Miss Churm was greatly in demand, never in want of employment, so I had no scruple in putting her off occasionally, to try them more at my ease. It was certainly amusing at first to do the real thing—it was amusing to do Major Monarch's trousers. They *were* the real thing, even if he did come out colossal. It was amusing to do his wife's back hair—it was so mathematically neat—and the particular "smart" tension of her tight stays. She lent herself especially to positions in which the face was somewhat averted or blurred, she abounded in ladylike back views and *profils perdus*. When she stood erect she took naturally one of the attitudes in which court-painters represent queens and princesses; so that I found myself wondering whether, to draw out this accomplishment, I couldn't get the editor of the *Cheapside* to publish a really royal romance, "A Tale of Buckingham Palace." Sometimes however the real thing and the make-believe came into contact; by which I mean that Miss Churm, keeping an appointment or coming to make one on days when I had much work in hand, encountered her invidious rivals. The encounter was not on their part, for they noticed her no more than if she had been the housemaid; not from intentional loftiness, but simply because as yet, professionally, they didn't know how to fraternise, as I could imagine they would have liked—or at least that the Major would. They couldn't talk about the omnibus—they always walked; and they didn't know what else to try—she wasn't interested in good trains or cheap claret. Besides, they must have felt—in the air—that she was amused at them, secretly derisive of their ever knowing how. She wasn't a person to conceal the limits of her faith if she had had a chance to show them. On the other hand Mrs. Monarch didn't think her tidy; for why else did she take pains to say to me—it was going out of the way, for Mrs. Monarch—that she didn't like dirty women?

One day when my young lady happened to be present with my other sitters—she even dropped in, when it was convenient, for a chat—I asked her to be so good as to lend a hand in getting tea, a service with which she was familiar and which was one of a class that, living as I did in a small way, with slender domestic resources, I often appealed to my models to render. They liked to lay hands on my property, to break the sitting, and sometimes the china—it made them feel Bohemian. The next time I saw Miss Churm after this incident she surprised me greatly by making a scene about it—she accused me of having wished to humiliate her. She hadn't resented the outrage at the time, but had seemed obliging and amused, enjoying the comedy of asking Mrs. Monarch, who sat vague and silent, whether she would have cream and sugar, and putting an exaggerated simper into the question. She had tried intonations—as if she too wished to pass for the real thing—till I was afraid my other visitors would take offence.

Oh they were determined not to do this, and their touching patience was the measure of their great need. They would sit by the hour, uncomplaining, till I was ready to use them; they would come back on the chance of being wanted and would walk away cheerfully if it failed. I used to go to the door with them to see in what magnificent order they retreated. I tried to find other employment for them—I introduced them to several artists. But they didn't "take," for reasons I could appreciate, and I became rather anxiously aware that after such disappointments they fell back upon me with a heavier weight. They did me the honour to think me most their form. They weren't romantic enough for the painters, and in those days there were few serious workers in black-and-white.

Besides, they had an eye to the great job I had mentioned to them—they had secretly set their hearts on supplying the right essence for my pictorial vindication of our fine novelist. They knew that for this undertaking I should want no costume—effects, none of the frippery of past ages—that it was a case in which everything would be contemporary and satirical and presumably genteel. If I could work them into it their future would be assured, for the labour would of course be long and the occupation steady.

One day Mrs. Monarch came without her husband—she explained his absence by his having had to go to the City. While she sat there in her usual relaxed majesty there came at the door a knock which I immediately recognised as the subdued appeal of a model out of work. It was followed by the entrance of a young man whom I at once saw to be a foreigner and who proved in fact an Italian acquainted with no English word but my name, which he uttered in a way that made it seem to include all others. I hadn't then visited his country, nor was I proficient in his tongue; but as he was not so meanly constituted—what Italian is?—as to depend only on that member for expression he conveyed to me, in familiar but graceful mimicry, that he was in search of exactly the employment in which the lady before me was engaged. I was not struck with him at first, and while I continued to draw I dropped few signs of interest or encouragement. He stood his ground however—not importunately, but with a dumb dog-like fidelity in his eyes that amounted to innocent impudence, the manner of a devoted servant—he might have been in the house for years—unjustly suspected. Suddenly it struck me that this very attitude and expression made a picture; whereupon I told him to sit down and wait till I should be free. There was another picture in the way he obeyed me, and I observed as I worked that there were others still in the way he looked wonderingly, with his head thrown back, about the high studio. He might have been crossing himself in Saint Peter's. Before I finished I said to myself "The fellow's a bankrupt orange-monger, but a treasure."

When Mrs. Monarch withdrew he passed across the room like a flash to open the door for her, standing there with the rapt pure gaze of the young Dante spellbound by the young Beatrice. As I never insisted, in such situations, on the blankness of the British domestic, I reflected that he had the making of a servant—and I needed one, but couldn't pay him to be only that—as well as of a model; in short I resolved to adopt my bright adventurer if he would agree to officiate in the double capacity. He jumped at my offer, and in the event my rashness—for I had really known nothing about him—wasn't brought home to me. He proved a sympathetic though a desultory ministrant, and had in a wonderful degree the *sentiment de la pose*. It was uncultivated, instinctive, a part of the happy instinct that had guided him to my door and helped him to spell out my name on the card nailed to it. He had had no other introduction to me than a guess, from the shape of my high north window, seen outside, that my place was a studio and that as a studio it would contain an artist. He had wandered to England in search of fortune, like other itinerants, and had embarked, with a partner and a small green hand-cart, on the sale of penny ices. The ices had melted away and the partner had dissolved in their train. My young man wore tight yellow trousers with reddish stripes and his name was Oronte. He was sallow but fair, and when I put him into some old clothes of my own he looked like an Englishman. He was as good as Miss Churm, who could look, when requested, like an Italian.

CHAPTER IV

I thought Mrs. Monarch's face slightly convulsed when, on her coming back with her husband, she found Oronte installed. It was strange to have to recognise in a scrap of a lazzarone a competitor to her magnificent Major. It was she who scented danger first, for the Major was anecdotically unconscious. But Oronte gave us tea, with a hundred eager confusions—he had never been concerned in so queer a process—and I think she thought better of me for having at last an "establishment." They saw a couple of drawings that I had made of the establishment, and Mrs. Monarch hinted that it never would have struck her he had sat for them. "Now the drawings you make from US, they look exactly like us," she reminded me, smiling in triumph; and I recognised that this was indeed just their defect. When I drew the Monarchs I couldn't anyhow get away from them—get into the character I wanted to represent; and I hadn't the least desire my model should be discoverable in my picture. Miss Churm never was, and Mrs. Monarch thought I hid her, very properly, because she was vulgar; whereas if she was lost it was only as the dead who go to heaven are lost—in the gain of an angel the more.

By this time I had got a certain start with "Rutland Ramsay," the first novel in the great projected series; that is I had produced a dozen drawings, several with the help of the Major and his wife, and I had sent them in for approval. My understanding with the publishers as I have already hinted, had been that I was to be left to do my work, in this particular case, as I liked, with the whole book committed to me; but my connexion with the rest of the series was only contingent. There were moments when, frankly, it *was* a comfort to have the real thing under one's hand for there were characters in "Rutland Ramsay" that were very much like it. There were people presumably as erect as the Major and women of as good a fashion as Mrs. Monarch. There was a great deal of country-house life-treated, it is true, in a fine fanciful ironical generalised way—and there was a considerable implication of knickerbockers and kilts. There were certain things I had to settle at the outset; such things for instance as the exact appearance of the hero and the particular bloom and figure of the heroine. The author of course gave me a lead, but there was a margin for interpretation. I took the Monarchs into my confidence, I told them frankly what I was about, I mentioned my embarrassments and alternatives. "Oh take *him!*" Mrs. Monarch murmured sweetly, looking at her husband; and "What could you want better than my wife?" the Major inquired with the comfortable candour that now prevailed between us.

I wasn't obliged to answer these remarks—I was only obliged to place my sitters. I wasn't easy in mind, and I postponed a little timidly perhaps the solving of my question. The book was a large canvas, the other figures were numerous, and I worked off at first some of the episodes in which the hero and the heroine were not concerned. When once I had set *them* up I should have to stick to them—I couldn't make my young man seven feet high in one place and five feet nine in another. I inclined on the whole to the latter measurement, though the Major more than once reminded me that he looked about as young as any one. It was indeed quite possible to arrange him, for the figure, so that it would have been difficult to detect his age. After the spontaneous Oronte had been with me a month, and after I had given him to understand several times over that his native exuberance would presently constitute an insurmountable barrier to our further intercourse, I waked to a sense of his heroic capacity. He was only five feet seven, but the remaining inches were latent. I tried him almost secretly at first, for I was really rather afraid of the judgement my other models would pass on such a choice. If they regarded Miss Churm as little better than a snare what would they think of the representation by a person so little the real thing as an Italian street-vendor of a protagonist formed by a public school?

If I went a little in fear of them it wasn't because they bullied me, because they had got an oppressive foothold, but because in their really pathetic decorum and mysteriously permanent newness they counted on me so intensely. I was therefore very glad when Jack Hawley came home: he was always of such good counsel. He painted badly himself, but there was no one like him for putting his finger on the place. He had been absent from England for a year; he had been somewhere—I don't remember where—to get a fresh eye. I was in a good deal of dread of any such organ, but we were old friends;

he had been away for months and a sense of emptiness was creeping into my life. I hadn't dodged a missile for a year.

He came back with a fresh eye, but with the same old black velvet blouse, and the first evening he spent in my studio we smoked cigarettes till the small hours. He had done no work himself, he had only got the eye; so the field was clear for the production of my little things. He wanted to see what I had produced for the *Cheapside*, but he was disappointed in the exhibition. That at least seemed the meaning of two or three comprehensive groans which, as he lounged on my big divan, his leg folded under him, looking at my latest drawings, issued from his lips with the smoke of the cigarette.

"What's the matter with you?" I asked.

"What's the matter with you?"

"Nothing save that I'm mystified."

"You are indeed. You're quite off the hinge. What's the meaning of this new fad?" And he tossed me, with visible irreverence, a drawing in which I happened to have depicted both my elegant models. I asked if he didn't think it good, and he replied that it struck him as execrable, given the sort of thing I had always represented myself to him as wishing to arrive at; but I let that pass—I was so anxious to see exactly what he meant. The two figures in the picture looked colossal, but I supposed this was not what he meant, inasmuch as, for aught he knew to the contrary, I might have been trying for some such effect. I maintained that I was working exactly in the same way as when he last had done me the honour to tell me I might do something some day. "Well, there's a screw loose somewhere," he answered; "wait a bit and I'll discover it." I depended upon him to do so: where else was the fresh eye? But he produced at last nothing more luminous than "I don't know—I don't like your types." This was lame for a critic who had never consented to discuss with me anything but the question of execution, the direction of strokes and the mystery of values.

"In the drawings you've been looking at I think my types are very handsome."

"Oh they won't do!"

"I've been working with new models."

"I see you have. *They* won't do."

"Are you very sure of that?"

"Absolutely—they're stupid."

"You mean I am—for I ought to get round that."

"You can't—with such people. Who are they?"

I told him, so far as was necessary, and he concluded heartlessly: *"Ce sont des gens qu'il faut mettre a la porte."*

"You've never seen them; they're awfully good"—I flew to their defence.

"Not seen them? Why all this recent work of yours drops to pieces with them. It's all I want to see of them."

"No one else has said anything against it—the *Cheapside* people are pleased."

"Every one else is an ass, and the *Cheapside* people the biggest asses of all. Come, don't pretend at this time of day to have pretty illusions about the public, especially about publishers and editors. It's not for *such* animals you work—it's for those who know, *coloro che sanno*; so keep straight for me if you can't keep straight for yourself. There was a certain sort of thing you used to try for—and a very good thing it was. But this twaddle isn't in it." When I talked with Hawley later about "Rutland Ramsay" and its possible successors he declared that I must get back into my boat again or I should go to the bottom. His voice in short was the voice of warning.

I noted the warning, but I didn't turn my friends out of doors. They bored me a good deal; but the very fact that they bored me admonished me not to sacrifice them—if there was anything to be done with them—simply to irritation. As I look back at this phase they seem to me to have pervaded my life not a little. I have a vision of them as most of the time in my studio, seated against the wall on an old velvet bench to be out of the way, and resembling the while a pair of patient courtiers in a royal antechamber. I'm convinced that during the coldest weeks of the winter they held their ground because it saved them fire. Their newness was losing its gloss, and it was impossible not to feel them objects of charity. Whenever Miss Churm arrived they went away, and after I was fairly launched in "Rutland Ramsay" Miss Churm arrived pretty often. They managed to express to me tacitly that they supposed I wanted her for the low life of the book, and I let them suppose it, since they had attempted to study the work—it was lying about the studio—without discovering that it dealt only with the highest circles. They had dipped into the most brilliant of our novelists without deciphering many passages. I still took an hour from them, now and again, in spite of Jack Hawley's warning: it would be time enough to dismiss them, if dismissal should be necessary, when the rigour of the season was over. Hawley had made their acquaintance—he had met them at my fireside—and thought them a ridiculous pair. Learning that he was a painter they tried to approach him, to show him too that they were the real thing; but he looked at them across the big room, as if they were miles away: they were a compendium of everything he most objected to in the social system of his country. Such people as that, all convention and patent-leather, with ejaculations that stopped conversation, had no business in a studio. A studio was a place to learn to see, and how could you see through a pair of feather-beds?

The main inconvenience I suffered at their hands was that at first I was shy of letting it break upon them that my artful little servant had begun to sit to me for "Rutland Ramsay." They knew I had been odd enough—they were prepared by this time to allow oddity to artists—to pick a foreign vagabond out of the streets when I might have had a person with whiskers and credentials; but it was some time before they learned how high I rated his accomplishments. They found him in an attitude more than once, but they never doubted I was doing him as an organ-grinder. There were several things they never guessed, and one of them was that for a striking scene in the novel, in which a footman briefly figured, it occurred to me to make use of Major Monarch as the menial. I kept putting this off, I didn't like to ask him to don the livery—besides the difficulty of finding a livery to fit him. At last, one day late in the winter, when I was at work on the despised Oronte, who caught one's idea on the wing, and was in the glow of feeling myself go very straight, they came in, the Major and his wife, with their society laugh about nothing (there was less and less to laugh at); came in like country-callers—they always reminded me of that—who have walked across the park after church and are presently persuaded to stay to luncheon. Luncheon was over, but they could stay to tea—I knew they wanted it. The fit was on me, however, and I couldn't let my ardour cool and my work wait, with the fading daylight, while my model prepared it. So I asked Mrs. Monarch if she would mind laying it out—a request which for an instant brought all the blood to her face. Her eyes were on her husband's for a second, and some mute telegraphy passed between them. Their folly was over the next instant; his cheerful shrewdness put an end to it. So far from pitying their wounded pride, I must add, I was moved to give it as complete a lesson as I could. They bustled about together and got out the cups and saucers and made the kettle boil. I know they felt as if they were waiting on my servant, and when the tea was prepared I said: "He'll have a cup, please—he's tired." Mrs. Monarch brought him one where he stood, and he took it from her as if he had been a gentleman at a party squeezing a crush-hat with an elbow.

Then it came over me that she had made a great effort for me—made it with a kind of nobleness—and that I owed her a compensation. Each time I saw her after this I wondered what the compensation could be. I couldn't go on doing the wrong thing to oblige them. Oh it *was* the wrong thing, the stamp of the work for which they sat—Hawley was not the only person to say it now. I sent in a large number of the drawings I had made for "Rutland Ramsay," and I received a warning that was more to the point than Hawley's. The artistic adviser of the house for which I was working was of opinion that many of my illustrations were not what had been looked for. Most of these illustrations were the subjects in which the Monarchs had figured. Without going into the question of what *had* been looked for, I had to face the fact that at this rate I shouldn't get the other books to do. I hurled myself in despair on Miss Churm—I put her through all her paces. I not only adopted Oronte publicly as my hero, but one morning when the Major looked in to see if I didn't require him to finish a *Cheapside* figure for which he had begun to sit the week before, I told him I had changed my mind—I'd do the drawing from my man. At this my visitor turned pale and stood looking at me. "Is HE your idea of an English gentleman?" he asked.

I was disappointed, I was nervous, I wanted to get on with my work; so. I replied with irritation: "Oh my dear Major—I can't be ruined for *you*!"

It was a horrid speech, but he stood another moment—after which, without a word, he quitted the studio. I drew a long breath, for I said to myself that I shouldn't see him again. I hadn't told him definitely that I was in danger of having my work rejected, but I was vexed at his not having felt the catastrophe in the air, read with me the moral of our fruitless collaboration, the lesson that in the deceptive atmosphere of art even the highest respectability may fail of being plastic.

I didn't owe my friends money, but I did see them again. They reappeared together three days later, and, given all the other facts, there was something tragic in that one. It was a clear proof they could find nothing else in life to do. They had threshed the matter out in a dismal conference—they had digested the bad news that they were not in for the series. If they weren't useful to me even for the *Cheapside* their function seemed difficult to determine, and I could only judge at first that they had come, forgivingly, decorously, to take a last leave. This made me rejoice in secret that I had little leisure for a scene; for I had placed both my other models in position together and I was pegging away at a drawing from which I hoped to derive glory. It had been suggested by the passage in which Rutland Ramsay, drawing up a chair to Artemisia's piano-stool, says extraordinary things to her while she ostensibly fingers out a difficult piece of music. I had done Miss Churm at the piano before—it was an attitude in which she knew how to take on an absolutely poetic grace. I wished the two figures to "compose" together with intensity, and my little Italian had entered perfectly into my conception. The pair were vividly before me, the piano had been pulled out; it was a charming show of blended youth and murmured love, which I had only to catch and keep. My visitors stood and looked at it, and I was friendly to them over my shoulder.

53

They made no response, but I was used to silent company and went on with my work, only a little disconcerted—even though exhilarated by the sense that this was at least the ideal thing—at not having got rid of them after all. Presently I heard Mrs. Monarch's sweet voice beside or rather above me: "I wish her hair were a little better done." I looked up and she was staring with a strange fixedness at Miss Churm, whose back was turned to her. "Do you mind my just touching it?" she went on—a question which made me spring up for an instant as with the instinctive fear that she might do the young lady a harm. But she quieted me with a glance I shall never forget—I confess I should like to have been able to paint that—and went for a moment to my model. She spoke to her softly, laying a hand on her shoulder and bending over her; and as the girl, understanding, gratefully assented, she disposed her rough curls, with a few quick passes, in such a way as to make Miss Churm's head twice as charming. It was one of the most heroic personal services I've ever seen rendered. Then Mrs. Monarch turned away with a low sigh and, looking about her as if for something to do, stooped to the floor with a noble humility and picked up a dirty rag that had dropped out of my paint-box.

The Major meanwhile had also been looking for something to do, and, wandering to the other end of the studio, saw before him my breakfast-things neglected, unremoved. "I say, can't I be useful *here*?" he called out to me with an irrepressible quaver. I assented with a laugh that I fear was awkward, and for the next ten minutes, while I worked, I heard the light clatter of china and the tinkle of spoons and glass. Mrs. Monarch assisted her husband—they washed up my crockery, they put it away. They wandered off into my little scullery, and I afterwards found that they had cleaned my knives and that my slender stock of plate had an unprecedented surface. When it came over me, the latent eloquence of what they were doing, I confess that my drawing was blurred for a moment—the picture swam. They had accepted their failure, but they couldn't accept their fate. They had bowed their heads in bewilderment to the perverse and cruel law in virtue of which the real thing could be so much less precious than the unreal; but they didn't want to starve. If my servants were my models, then my models might be my servants. They would reverse the parts—the others would sit for the ladies and gentlemen and *they* would do the work. They would still be in the studio—it was an intense dumb appeal to me not to turn them out. "Take us on," they wanted to say—"we'll do *anything*."

My pencil dropped from my hand; my sitting was spoiled and I got rid of my sitters, who were also evidently rather mystified and awestruck. Then, alone with the Major and his wife I had a most uncomfortable moment. He put their prayer into a single sentence: "I say, you know—just let US do for you, can't you?" I couldn't—it was dreadful to see them emptying my slops; but I pretended I could, to oblige them, for about a week. Then I gave them a sum of money to go away, and I never saw them again. I obtained the remaining books, but my friend Hawley repeats that Major and Mrs. Monarch did me a permanent harm, got me into false ways. If it be true I'm content to have paid the price—for the memory.

THE STORY OF IT

CHAPTER I

The weather had turned so much worse that the rest of the day was certainly lost. The wind had risen and the storm gathered force; they gave from time to time a thump at the firm windows and dashed even against those protected by the verandah their vicious splotches of rain. Beyond the lawn, beyond the cliff, the great wet brush of the sky dipped deep into the sea. But the lawn, already vivid with the touch of May, showed a violence of watered green; the budding shrubs and trees repeated the note as they tossed their thick masses, and the cold troubled light, filling the pretty saloon, marked the spring afternoon as sufficiently young. The two ladies seated there in silence could pursue without difficulty—as well as, clearly, without interruption—their respective tasks; a confidence expressed, when the noise of the wind allowed it to be heard, by the sharp scratch of Mrs. Dyott's pen at the table where she was busy with letters.

Her visitor, settled on a small sofa that, with a palm-tree, a screen, a stool, a stand, a bowl of flowers and three photographs in silver frames, had been arranged near the light wood-fire as a choice "corner"—Maud Blessingbourne, her guest, turned audibly, though at intervals neither brief nor regular, the leaves of a book covered in lemon-coloured paper and not yet despoiled of a certain fresh crispness. This effect of the volume, for the eye, would have made it, as presumably the newest French novel—and evidently, from the attitude of the reader, "good"—consort happily with the special tone of the room, a consistent air of selection and suppression, one of the finer aesthetic evolutions. If Mrs. Dyott was fond of ancient French furniture and distinctly difficult about it, her inmates could be fond—with whatever critical cocks of charming dark-braided heads over slender sloping shoulders—of modern French authors. Nothing had passed for half an hour—nothing at least, to be exact, but that each of the companions occasionally and covertly intermitted her pursuit in such a manner as to ascertain the degree of absorption of the other without turning round. What their silence was charged with therefore was not only a sense of the weather, but a sense, so to speak, of its own nature. Maud Blessingbourne, when she lowered her book into her lap, closed her eyes with a conscious patience that seemed to say she waited; but it was nevertheless she who at last made the movement representing a snap of their tension. She got up and stood by the fire, into which she looked a minute; then came round and approached the window as if to see what was really going on. At this Mrs. Dyott wrote with refreshed intensity. Her little pile of letters had grown, and if a look of determination was compatible with her fair and slightly faded beauty, the habit of attending to her business could always keep pace with any excursion of her thought. Yet she was the first who spoke.

"I trust your book has been interesting."

"Well enough; a little mild."

A louder throb of the tempest had blurred the sound of the words. "A little wild?"

"Dear no—timid and tame; unless I've quite lost my sense."

"Perhaps you have," Mrs. Dyott placidly suggested—"reading so many."

Her companion made a motion of feigned despair. "Ah you take away my courage for going to my room, as I was just meaning to, for another."

"Another French one?"

"I'm afraid."

"Do you carry them by the dozen—?"

"Into innocent British homes?" Maud tried to remember. "I believe I brought three—seeing them in a shop-window as I passed through town. It never rains but it pours! But I've already read two."

"And are they the only ones you do read?"

"French ones?" Maud considered. "Oh no. D'Annunzio."

"And what's that?" Mrs. Dyott asked as she affixed a stamp.

"Oh you dear thing!" Her friend was amused, yet almost showed pity. "I know you don't read," Maud went on; "but why should you? *You* live!"

"Yes—wretchedly enough," Mrs. Dyott returned, getting her letters together. She left her place, holding them as a neat achieved handful, and came over to the fire, while Mrs. Blessingbourne turned once more to the window, where she was met by another flurry.

Maud spoke then as if moved only by the elements. "Do you expect him through all this?"

Mrs. Dyott just waited, and it had the effect, indescribably, of making everything that had gone before seem to have led up to the question. This effect was even deepened by the way she then said "Whom do you mean?"

"Why I thought you mentioned at luncheon that Colonel Voyt was to walk over. Surely he can't."

"Do you care very much?" Mrs. Dyott asked.

Her friend now hesitated. "It depends on what you call 'much.' If you mean should I like to see him—then certainly."

"Well, my dear, I think he understands you're here."

"So that as he evidently isn't coming," Maud laughed, "it's particularly flattering! Or rather," she added, giving up the prospect again, "it would be, I think, quite extraordinarily flattering if he did. Except that of course," she threw in, "he might come partly for you."

"'Partly' is charming. Thank you for 'partly.' If you *are* going upstairs, will you kindly," Mrs Dyott pursued, "put these into the box as you pass?"

The younger woman, taking the little pile of letters, considered them with envy. "Nine! You *are* good. You're always a living reproach!"

Mrs. Dyott gave a sigh. "I don't do it on purpose. The only thing, this afternoon," she went on, reverting to the other question, "would be their not having come down."

"And as to that you don't know."

"No—I don't know." But she caught even as she spoke a rat-tat-tat of the knocker, which struck her as a sign. "Ah there!"

"Then I go." And Maud whisked out.

Mrs. Dyott, left alone, moved with an air of selection to the window, and it was as so stationed, gazing out at the wild weather, that the visitor, whose delay to appear spoke of the wiping of boots and the disposal of drenched mackintosh and cap, finally found her. He was tall lean fine, with little in him, on the whole, to confirm the titular in the "Colonel Voyt" by which he was announced. But he had left the army, so that his reputation for gallantry mainly depended now on his fighting Liberalism in the House of Commons. Even these facts, however, his aspect scantily matched; partly, no doubt, because he looked, as was usually said, un-English. His black hair, cropped close, was lightly powdered with silver, and his dense glossy beard, that of an emir or a caliph, and grown for civil reasons, repeated its handsome colour and its somewhat foreign effect. His nose had a strong and shapely arch, and the dark grey of his eyes was tinted with blue. It had been said of him—in relation to these signs—that he would have struck you as a Jew had he not, in spite of his nose, struck you so much as an Irishman. Neither responsibility could in fact have been fixed upon him, and just now, at all events, he was only a pleasant weather-washed wind-battered Briton, who brought in from a struggle with the elements that he appeared quite to have enjoyed a certain amount of unremoved mud and an unusual quantity of easy expression. It was exactly the silence ensuing on the retreat of the servant and the closed door that marked between him and his hostess the degree of this ease. They met, as it were, twice: the first time while the servant was there and the second as soon as he was not. The difference was great between the two encounters, though we must add in justice to the second that its marks were at first mainly negative. This communion consisted only in their having drawn each other for a minute as close as possible—as possible, that is, with no help but the full clasp of hands. Thus they were mutually held, and the closeness was at any rate such that, for a little, though it took account of dangers, it did without words. When words presently came the pair were talking by the fire and she had rung for tea. He had by this time asked if the note he had despatched to her after breakfast had been safely delivered.

"Yes, before luncheon. But I'm always in a state when—except for some extraordinary reason—you send such things by hand. I knew, without it, that you had come. It never fails. I'm sure when you're there—I'm sure when you're not."

He wiped, before the glass, his wet moustache. "I see. But this morning I had an impulse."

"It was beautiful. But they make me as uneasy, sometimes, your impulses, as if they were calculations; make me wonder what you have in reserve."

"Because when small children are too awfully good they die? Well, I AM a small child compared to you—but I'm not dead yet. I cling to life."

He had covered her with his smile, but she continued grave. "I'm not half so much afraid when you're nasty."

"Thank you! What then did you do," he asked, "with my note?"

"You deserve that I should have spread it out on my dressing-table—or left it, better still, in Maud Blessingbourne's room."

He wondered while he laughed. "Oh but what does *she* deserve?"

It was her gravity that continued to answer. "Yes—it would probably kill her."

"She believes so in you?"

"She believes so in *you*. So don't be *too* nice to her."

He was still looking, in the chimney-glass, at the state of his beard—brushing from it, with his handkerchief, the traces of wind and wet. "If she also then prefers me when I'm nasty it seems to me I ought to satisfy her. Shall I now at any rate see her?"

"She's so like a pea on a pan over the possibility of it that she's pulling herself together in her room."

"Oh then we must try and keep her together. But why, graceful, tender, pretty too—quite or almost as she is—doesn't she re-marry?"

Mrs. Dyott appeared—and as if the first time—to look for the reason. "Because she likes too many men."

It kept up his spirits. "And how many *may* a lady like—?"

"In order not to like any of them too much? Ah that, you know, I never found out—and it's too late now. When," she presently pursued, "did you last see her?"

He really had to think. "Would it have been since last November or so?—somewhere or other where we spent three days."

"Oh at Surredge? I know all about that. I thought you also met afterwards."

He had again to recall. "So we did! Wouldn't it have been somewhere at Christmas? But it wasn't by arrangement!" he laughed, giving with his forefinger a little pleasant nick to his hostess's chin. Then as if something in the way she received this attention put him back to his question of a moment before: "Have you kept my note?"

She held him with her pretty eyes. "Do you want it back?"

"Ah don't speak as if I did take things—!"

She dropped her gaze to the fire. "No, you don't; not even the hard things a really generous nature often would." She quitted, however, as if to forget that, the chimney-place. "I put it *there*!"

"You've burnt it? Good!" It made him easier, but he noticed the next moment on a table the lemon-coloured volume left there by Mrs.

Blessingbourne, and, taking it up for a look, immediately put it down. "You might while you were about it have burnt that too."

"You've read it?"

"Dear yes. And you?"

"No," said Mrs. Dyott; "it wasn't for me Maud brought it."

It pulled her visitor up. "Mrs. Blessingbourne brought it?"

"For such a day as this." But she wondered. "How you look! Is it so awful?"

"Oh like his others." Something had occurred to him; his thought was already far. "Does she know?"

"Know what?"

"Why anything."

But the door opened too soon for Mrs. Dyott, who could only murmur quickly—"Take care!"

CHAPTER II

It was in fact Mrs. Blessingbourne, who had under her arm the book she had gone up for—a pair of covers showing this time a pretty, a candid blue. She was followed next minute by the servant, who brought in tea, the consumption of which, with the passage of greetings, inquiries and other light civilities between the two visitors, occupied a quarter of an hour. Mrs. Dyott meanwhile, as a contribution to so much amenity, mentioned to Maud that her fellow guest wished to scold her for the books she read—a statement met by this friend with the remark that he must first be sure about them. But as soon as he had picked up the new, the blue volume he broke out into a frank "Dear, dear!"

"Have you read that too?" Mrs. Dyott inquired. "How much you'll have to talk over together! The other one," she explained to him, "Maud speaks of as terribly tame."

"Ah I must have that out with her! You don't feel the extraordinary force of the fellow?" Voyt went on to Mrs. Blessingbourne.

And so, round the hearth, they talked—talked soon, while they warmed their toes, with zest enough to make it seem as happy a chance as any of the quieter opportunities their imprisonment might have involved. Mrs. Blessingbourne did feel, it then appeared, the force of the fellow, but she had her reserves and reactions, in which Voyt was much interested. Mrs. Dyott rather detached herself, mainly gazing, as she leaned back, at the fire; she intervened, however, enough to relieve Maud of the sense of being listened to. That sense, with Maud, was too apt to convey that one was listened to for a fool. "Yes, when I read a novel I mostly read a French one," she had said to Voyt in answer to a question about her usual practice; "for I seem with it to get hold more of the real thing—to get more life for my money. Only I'm not so infatuated with them but that sometimes for months and months on end I don't read any fiction at all."

The two books were now together beside them. "Then when you begin again you read a mass?"

"Dear no. I only keep up with three or four authors."

He laughed at this over the cigarette he had been allowed to light. "I like your 'keeping up,' and keeping up in particular with 'authors.'"

"One must keep up with somebody," Mrs. Dyott threw off.

"I daresay I'm ridiculous," Mrs. Blessingbourne conceded without heeding it; "but that's the way we express ourselves in my part of the country."

"I only alluded," said Voyt, "to the tremendous conscience of your sex. It's more than mine can keep up with. You take everything too hard. But if you can't read the novel of British and American manufacture, heaven knows I'm at one with you. It seems really to show our sense of life as the sense of puppies and kittens."

"Well," Maud more patiently returned, "I'm told all sorts of people are now doing wonderful things; but somehow I remain outside."

"Ah it's *they*, it's our poor twangers and twaddlers who remain outside. They pick up a living in the street. And who indeed would want them in?"

Mrs. Blessingbourne seemed unable to say, and yet at the same time to have her idea. The subject, in truth, she evidently found, was not so easy to handle. "People lend me things, and I try; but at the end of fifty pages—"

"There you are! Yes—heaven help us!"

"But what I mean," she went on, "isn't that I don't get woefully weary of the eternal French thing. What's *their* sense of life?"

"*Ah voilà!*" Mrs. Dyott softly sounded.

"Oh but it IS one; you can make it out," Voyt promptly declared. "They do what they feel, and they feel more things than we. They strike so many more notes, and with so different a hand. When it comes to any account of a relation say between a man and a woman—I mean an intimate or a curious or a suggestive one—where are we compared to them? They don't exhaust the subject, no doubt," he admitted; "but we don't touch it, don't even skim it. It's as if we denied its existence, its possibility. You'll doubtless tell me, however," he went on, "that as all such relations *are* for us at the most much simpler we can only have all round less to say about them."

She met this imputation with the quickest amusement. "I beg your pardon. I don't think I shall tell you anything of the sort. I don't know that I even agree with your premiss."

"About such relations?" He looked agreeably surprised. "You think we make them larger?—or subtler?"

Mrs. Blessingbourne leaned back, not looking, like Mrs. Dyott, at the fire, but at the ceiling. "I don't know what I think."

"It's not that she doesn't know," Mrs. Dyott remarked. "It's only that she doesn't say."

But Voyt had this time no eye for their hostess. For a moment he watched Maud. "It sticks out of you, you know, that you've yourself written something. Haven't you—and published? I've a notion I could read *you*."

"When I do publish," she said without moving, "you'll be the last one I shall tell. I *have*," she went on, "a lovely subject, but it would take an amount of treatment—!"

"Tell us then at least what it is."

At this she again met his eyes. "Oh to tell it would be to express it, and that's just what I can't do. What I meant to say just now," she added, "was that the French, to my sense, give us only again and again, for ever and ever, the same couple. There they are once more, as one has had them to satiety, in that yellow thing, and there I shall certainly again find them in the blue."

"Then why do you keep reading about them?" Mrs. Dyott demanded.

Maud cast about. "I don't!" she sighed. "At all events, I shan't any more. I give it up."

"You've been looking for something, I judge," said Colonel Voyt, "that you're not likely to find. It doesn't exist."

"What is it?" Mrs. Dyott desired to know.

"I never look," Maud remarked, "for anything but an interest."

"Naturally. But your interest," Voyt replied, "is in something different from life."

"Ah not a bit! I *love* life in art, though I hate it anywhere else. It's the poverty of the life those people show, and the awful bounders, of both sexes, that they represent."

"Oh now we have you!" her interlocutor laughed. "To me, when all's said and done, they seem to be—as near as art can come—in the truth of the truth. It can only take what life gives it, though it certainly may be a pity that that isn't better. Your complaint of their monotony is a complaint of their conditions. When you say we get always the same couple what do you mean but that we get always the same passion? Of course we do!" Voyt pursued. "If what you're looking for is another, that's what you won't anywhere find."

Maud for a while said nothing, and Mrs. Dyott seemed to wait. "Well, I suppose I'm looking, more than anything else, for a decent woman."

"Oh then you mustn't look for her in pictures of passion. That's not her element nor her whereabouts."

Mrs. Blessingbourne weighed the objection. "Does it not depend on what you mean by passion?"

"I think I can mean only one thing: the enemy to behaviour."

"Oh I can imagine passions that are on the contrary friends to it."

Her fellow-guest thought. "Doesn't it depend perhaps on what you mean by behaviour?"

"Dear no. Behaviour's just behaviour—the most definite thing in the world."

"Then what do you mean by the 'interest' you just now spoke of? The picture of that definite thing?"

"Yes—call it that. Women aren't *always* vicious, even when they're—"

"When they're what?" Voyt pressed.

"When they're unhappy. They can be unhappy and good."

"That one doesn't for a moment deny. But can they be 'good' and interesting?"

"That must be Maud's subject!" Mrs. Dyott interposed. "To show a woman who IS. I'm afraid, my dear," she continued, "you could only show yourself."

"You'd show then the most beautiful specimen conceivable"—and Voyt addressed himself to Maud. "But doesn't it prove that life is, against your contention, more interesting than art? Life you embellish and elevate; but art would find itself able to do nothing with you, and, on such impossible terms, would ruin you."

The colour in her faint consciousness gave beauty to her stare. "'Ruin' me?"

"He means," Mrs. Dyott again indicated, "that you'd ruin 'art.'"

"Without on the other hand"—Voyt seemed to assent—"its giving at all a coherent impression of you."

"She wants her romance cheap!" said Mrs. Dyott.

"Oh no—I should be willing to pay for it. I don't see why the romance—since you give it that name—should be all, as the French inveterately make it, for the women who are bad."

"Oh they pay for it!" said Mrs. Dyott.

"DO they?"

"So at least"—Mrs. Dyott a little corrected herself—"one has gathered (for I don't read your books, you know!) that they're usually shown as doing."

Maud wondered, but looking at Voyt, "They're shown often, no doubt, as paying for their badness. But are they shown as paying for their romance?"

"My dear lady," said Voyt, "their romance is their badness. There isn't any other. It's a hard law, if you will, and a strange, but goodness has to go without that luxury. Isn't to BE good just exactly, all round, to go without?" He put it before her kindly and clearly—regretfully too, as if he were sorry the truth should be so sad. He and she, his pleasant eyes seemed to say, would, had they had the making of it, have made it better. "One has heard it before—at least I have; one has heard your question put. But always, when put to a mind not merely muddled, for an inevitable answer. 'Why don't you, *cher monsieur*, give us the drama of virtue?' 'Because, *chère madame*, the high privilege of virtue is precisely to avoid drama.' The adventures of the honest lady? The honest lady hasn't, can't possibly have, adventures."

Mrs. Blessingbourne only met his eyes at first, smiling with some intensity. "Doesn't it depend a little on what you call adventures?"

"My poor Maud," said Mrs. Dyott as if in compassion for sophistry so simple, "adventures are just adventures. That's all you can make of them!"

But her friend talked for their companion and as if without hearing. "Doesn't it depend a good deal on what you call drama?" Maud spoke as one who had already thought it out. "Doesn't it depend on what you call romance?"

Her listener gave these arguments his very best attention. "Of course you may call things anything you like—speak of them as one thing and mean quite another. But why should it depend on anything? Behind these words we use—the adventure, the novel, the drama, the romance, the situation, in short, as we most comprehensively say—behind them all stands the same sharp fact which they all in their different ways represent."

"Precisely!" Mrs. Dyott was full of approval.

Maud however was full of vagueness. "What great fact?"

"The fact of a relation. The adventure's a relation; the relation's an adventure. The romance, the novel, the drama are the picture of one. The subject the novelist treats is the rise, the formation, the development, the climax and for the most part the decline of one. And what is the honest lady doing on that side of the town?"

Mrs. Dyott was more pointed. "She doesn't so much as *form* a relation."

But Maud bore up. "Doesn't it depend again on what you call a relation?"

"Oh," said Mrs. Dyott, "if a gentleman picks up her pocket-handkerchief—"

"Ah even that's one," their friend laughed, "if she has thrown it to him. We can only deal with one that is one."

"Surely," Maud replied. "But if it's an innocent one—"

"Doesn't it depend a good deal," Mrs. Dyott asked, "on what you call innocent?"

"You mean that the adventures of innocence have so often been the material of fiction? Yes," Voyt replied; "that's exactly what the bored reader complains of. He has asked for bread and been given a stone. What is it but, with absolute directness, a question of interest or, as people say, of the story? What's a situation undeveloped but a subject lost? If a relation stops, where's the story? If it doesn't stop, where's the innocence? It seems to me you must choose. It would be very pretty if it were otherwise, but that's how we flounder. Art is our flounderings shown."

Mrs. Blessingbourne—and with an air of deference scarce supported perhaps by its sketchiness—kept her deep eyes on this definition. "But sometimes we flounder out."

It immediately touched in Colonel Voyt the spring of a genial derision. "That's just where I expected *you* would! One always sees it come."

"He has, you notice," Mrs. Dyott parenthesised to Maud, "seen it come so often; and he has always waited for it and met it."

"Met it, dear lady, simply enough! It's the old story, Mrs. Blessingbourne. The relation's innocent that the heroine gets out of. The book's innocent that's the story of her getting out. But what the devil—in the name of innocence—was she doing IN?"

Mrs. Dyott promptly echoed the question. "You have to be in, you know, to *get* out. So there you are already with your relation. It's the end of your goodness."

"And the beginning," said Voyt, "of your play!"

"Aren't they all, for that matter, even the worst," Mrs. Dyott pursued, "supposed *some* time or other to get out? But if meanwhile they've been in, however briefly, long enough to adorn a tale?"

"They've been in long enough to point a moral. That is to point ours!" With which, and as if a sudden flush of warmer light had moved him, Colonel Voyt got up. The veil of the storm had parted over a great red sunset.

Mrs. Dyott also was on her feet, and they stood before his charming antagonist, who, with eyes lowered and a somewhat fixed smile, had not moved.

"We've spoiled her subject!" the elder lady sighed.

"Well," said Voyt, "it's better to spoil an artist's subject than to spoil his reputation. I mean," he explained to Maud with his indulgent manner, "his appearance of knowing what he has got hold of, for that, in the last resort, is his happiness."

She slowly rose at this, facing him with an aspect as handsomely mild as his own. "You can't spoil my happiness."

He held her hand an instant as he took leave. "I wish I could add to it!"

CHAPTER III

When he had quitted them and Mrs. Dyott had candidly asked if her friend had found him rude or crude, Maud replied—though not immediately—that she had feared showing only too much how charming she found him. But if Mrs. Dyott took this it was to weigh the sense. "How could you show it too much?"

"Because I always feel that that's my only way of showing anything. It's absurd, if you like," Mrs. Blessingbourne pursued, "but I never know, in such intense discussions, what strange impression I may give."

Her companion looked amused. "Was it intense?"

"*I* was," Maud frankly confessed.

"Then it's a pity you were so wrong. Colonel Voyt, you know, is right." Mrs. Blessingbourne at this gave one of the slow soft silent headshakes to which she often resorted and which, mostly accompanied by the light of cheer, had somehow, in spite of the small obstinacy that smiled in them, a special grace. With this grace, for a moment, her friend, looking her up and down, appeared impressed, yet not too much so to take the next minute a decision. "Oh my dear, I'm sorry to differ from any one so lovely—for you're awfully beautiful to-night, and your frock's the very nicest I've ever seen you wear. But he's as right as he can be."

Maud repeated her motion. "Not so right, at all events as he thinks he is. Or perhaps I can say," she went on, after an instant, "that I'm not so wrong. I do know a little what I'm talking about."

Mrs. Dyott continued to study her. "You *are* vexed. You naturally don't like it—such destruction."

"Destruction?"

"Of your illusion."

"I *have* no illusion. If I had moreover it wouldn't be destroyed. I have on the whole, I think, my little decency."

Mrs. Dyott stared. "Let us grant it for argument. What, then?"

"Well, I've also my little drama."

"An attachment?"

"An attachment."

"That you shouldn't have?"

"That I shouldn't have."

"A passion?"

"A passion."

"Shared?"

"Ah thank goodness, no!"

Mrs. Dyott continued to gaze. "The object's unaware—?"

"Utterly."

Mrs. Dyott turned it over. "Are you sure?"

"Sure."

"That's what you call your decency? But isn't it," Mrs. Dyott asked, "rather his?"

"Dear no. It's only his good fortune."

Mrs. Dyott laughed. "But yours, darling—your good fortune: where does *that* come in?"

"Why, in my sense of the romance of it."

"The romance of what? Of his not knowing?"

"Of my not wanting him to. If I did"—Maud had touchingly worked it out—"where would be my honesty?"

The inquiry, for an instant, held her friend, yet only, it seemed, for a stupefaction that was almost amusement. "Can you want or not want as you like? Where in the world, if you don't want, is your romance?"

Mrs. Blessingbourne still wore her smile, and she now, with a light gesture that matched it, just touched the region of her heart. "There!"

Her companion admiringly marvelled. "A lovely place for it, no doubt!— but not quite a place, that I can see, to make the sentiment a relation."

"Why not? What more is required for a relation for me?"

"Oh all sorts of things, I should say! And many more, added to those, to make it one for the person you mention."

"Ah that I don't pretend it either should be or *can* be. I only speak for myself."

This was said in a manner that made Mrs. Dyott, with a visible mixture of impressions, suddenly turn away. She indulged in a vague movement or two, as if to look for something; then again found herself near her friend, on whom with the same abruptness, in fact with a strange sharpness, she conferred a kiss that might have represented either her tribute to exalted consistency or her idea of a graceful close of the discussion. "You deserve that one should speak *for* you!"

Her companion looked cheerful and secure. "How *can* you without knowing—?"

"Oh by guessing! It's not—?"

But that was as far as Mrs. Dyott could get. "It's not," said Maud, "any one you've ever seen."

"Ah then I give you up!"

And Mrs. Dyott conformed for the rest of Maud's stay to the spirit of this speech. It was made on a Saturday night, and Mrs. Blessingbourne remained till the Wednesday following, an interval during which, as the return of fine weather was confirmed by the Sunday, the two ladies found a wider range of action. There were drives to be taken, calls made, objects of interest seen at a distance; with the effect of much easy talk and still more easy silence. There had been a question of Colonel Voyt's probable return on the Sunday, but the whole time passed without a sign from him, and it was merely mentioned by Mrs. Dyott, in explanation, that he must have been suddenly called, as he was so liable to be, to town. That this in fact was what had happened he made clear to her on Thursday afternoon, when, walking over again late, he found her alone. The consequence of his Sunday letters had been his taking, that day, the 4.15. Mrs. Voyt had gone back on Thursday, and he now, to settle on the spot the question of a piece of work begun at his place, had rushed down for a few hours in anticipation of the usual collective move for the week's end. He was to go up again by the late train, and had to count a little—a fact accepted by his hostess with the hard pliancy of practice—his present happy moments. Too few as these were, however, he found time to make of her an inquiry or two not directly bearing on their situation. The first was a recall of the question for which Mrs. Blessingbourne's entrance on the previous Saturday had arrested her answer. Had that lady the idea of anything between them?

"No. I'm sure. There's one idea she has got," Mrs. Dyott went on; "but it's quite different and not so very wonderful."

"What then is it?"

"Well, that she's herself in love."

Voyt showed his interest. "You mean she told you?"

"I got it out of her."

He showed his amusement. "Poor thing! And with whom?"

"With you."

His surprise, if the distinction might be made, was less than his wonder. "You got that out of her too?"

"No—it remains in. Which is much the best way for it. For you to know it would be to end it."

He looked rather cheerfully at sea. "Is that then why you tell me?"

"I mean for her to know you know it. Therefore it's in your interest not to let her."

"I see," Voyt after a moment returned. "Your real calculation is that my interest will be sacrificed to my vanity—so that, if your other idea is just, the flame will in fact, and thanks to her morbid conscience, expire by her taking fright at seeing me so pleased. But I promise you," he declared, "that she shan't see it. So there you are!" She kept her eyes on him and had evidently to admit after a little that there she was. Distinct as he had made the case, however, he wasn't yet quite satisfied. "Why are you so sure I'm the man?"

"From the way she denies you."

"You put it to her?"

"Straight. If you hadn't been she'd of course have confessed to you—to keep me in the dark about the real one."

Poor Voyt laughed out again. "Oh you dear souls!"

"Besides," his companion pursued, "I wasn't in want of that evidence."

"Then what other had you?"

"Her state before you came—which was what made me ask you how much you had seen her. And her state after it," Mrs. Dyott added. "And her state," she wound up, "while you were here."

"But her state while I was here was charming."

"Charming. That's just what I say."

She said it in a tone that placed the matter in its right light—a light in which they appeared kindly, quite tenderly, to watch Maud wander away into space with her lovely head bent under a theory rather too big for it. Voyt's last word, however, was that there was just enough in it—in the theory—for them to allow that she had not shown herself, on the occasion of their talk, wholly bereft of sense. Her consciousness, if they let it alone—as they of course after this mercifully must—*was*, in the last analysis, a kind of shy romance. Not a romance like their own, a thing to make the fortune of any author up to the mark—one who should have the invention or who *could* have the courage; but a small scared starved subjective satisfaction that would do her no harm and nobody else any good. Who but a duffer—he stuck to his contention—would see the shadow of a "story" in it?

FLICKERBRIDGE

CHAPTER I

Frank Granger had arrived from Paris to paint a portrait—an order given him, as a young compatriot with a future, whose early work would some day have a price, by a lady from New York, a friend of his own people and also, as it happened, of Addie's, the young woman to whom it was publicly both affirmed and denied that he was engaged. Other young women in Paris—fellow-members there of the little tight transpontine world of art-study—professed to know that the pair had "several times" over renewed their fond understanding. This, however, was their own affair; the last phase of the relation, the last time of the times, had passed into vagueness; there was perhaps even an impression that if they were inscrutable to their friends they were not wholly crystalline to each other and themselves. What had occurred for Granger at all events in connexion with the portrait was that Mrs. Bracken, his intending model, whose return to America was at hand, had suddenly been called to London by her husband, occupied there with pressing business, but had yet desired that her displacement should not interrupt her sittings. The young man, at her request, had followed her to England and profited by all she could give him, making shift with a small studio lent him by a London painter whom he had known and liked a few years before in the French atelier that then cradled, and that continued to cradle, so many of their kind.

The British capital was a strange grey world to him, where people walked, in more ways than one, by a dim light; but he was happily of such a turn that the impression, just as it came, could nowhere ever fail him, and even the worst of these things was almost as much an occupation—putting it only at that—as the best. Mrs. Bracken moreover passed him on, and while the darkness ebbed a little in the April days he found himself consolingly committed to a couple of fresh subjects. This cut him out work for more than another month, but meanwhile, as he said, he saw a lot—a lot that, with frequency and with much expression, he wrote about to Addie. She also wrote to her absent friend, but in briefer snatches, a meagreness to her reasons for which he had long since assented. She had other play for her pen as well as, fortunately, other remuneration; a regular correspondence for a "prominent Boston paper," fitful connexions with public sheets perhaps also in cases fitful, and a mind above all engrossed at times, to the exclusion of everything else, with the study of the short story. This last was what she had mainly come out to go into, two or three years after he had found himself engulfed in the mystery of Carolus. She was indeed, on her own deep sea, more engulfed than he had ever been, and he had grown to accept the sense that, for progress too, she sailed under more canvas. It hadn't been particularly present to him till now that he had in the least got on, but the way in which Addie had—and evidently still more would—was the theme, as it were, of every tongue. She had thirty short stories out and nine descriptive articles. His three or four portraits of fat American ladies—they were all fat, all ladies and all American—were a poor show compared with these triumphs; especially as Addie had begun to throw out that it was about time they should go home. It kept perpetually coming up in Paris, in the transpontine world, that, as the phrase was, America had grown more interesting since they left. Addie was attentive to the rumour, and, as full of conscience as she was of taste, of patriotism as of curiosity, had often put it to him frankly, with what he, who was of New York, recognised as her New England emphasis: "I'm not sure, you know, that we do *real* justice to our country." Granger felt he would do it on the day—if the day ever came—he should irrevocably marry her. No other country could possibly have produced her.

CHAPTER II

But meanwhile it befell that, in London, he was stricken with influenza and with subsequent sorrow. The attack was short but sharp—had it lasted Addie would certainly have come to his aid; most of a blight really in its secondary stage. The good ladies his sitters—the ladies with the frizzled hair, with the diamond earrings, with the chins tending to the massive—left for him, at the door of his lodgings, flowers, soup and love, so that with their assistance he pulled through; but his convalescence was slow and his weakness out of proportion to the muffled shock. He came out, but he went about lame; it tired him to paint—he felt as if he had been ill three months. He strolled in Kensington Gardens when he should have been at work; he sat long on penny chairs and helplessly mused and mooned. Addie desired him to return to Paris, but there were chances under his hand that he felt he had just wit enough left not to relinquish. He would have gone for a week to the sea—he would have gone to Brighton; but Mrs. Bracken had to be finished—Mrs. Bracken was so soon to sail. He just managed to finish her in time—the day before the date fixed for his breaking ground on a greater business still, the circumvallation of Mrs. Dunn. Mrs. Dunn duly waited on him, and he sat down before her, feeling, however, ere he rose, that he must take a long breath before the attack. While asking himself that night, therefore, where he should best replenish his lungs he received from Addie, who had had from Mrs. Bracken a poor report of him, a communication which, besides being of sudden and startling interest, applied directly to his case.

His friend wrote to him under the lively emotion of having from one day to another become aware of a new relative, an ancient cousin, a sequestered gentlewoman, the sole survival of "the English branch of the family," still resident, at Flickerbridge, in the "old family home," and with whom, that he might immediately betake himself to so auspicious a quarter for change of air, she had already done what was proper to place him, as she said, in touch. What came of it all, to be brief, was that Granger found himself so placed almost as he read: he was in touch with Miss Wenham of Flickerbridge, to

the extent of being in correspondence with her, before twenty-four hours had
sped. And on the second day he was in the train, settled for a five-hours' run
to the door of this amiable woman who had so abruptly and kindly taken
him on trust and of whom but yesterday he had never so much as heard.
This was an oddity—the whole incident was—of which, in the corner of his
compartment, as he proceeded, he had time to take the size. But the surprise,
the incongruity, as he felt, could but deepen as he went. It was a sufficiently
queer note, in the light, or the absence of it, of his late experience, that so
complex a product as Addie should have *any* simple insular tie; but it was
a queerer note still that she should have had one so long only to remain
unprofitably unconscious of it. Not to have done something with it, used it,
worked it, talked about it at least, and perhaps even written—these things,
at the rate she moved, represented a loss of opportunity under which as he
saw her, she was peculiarly formed to wince. She was at any rate, it was clear,
doing something with it now; using it, working it, certainly, already talking—
and, yes, quite possibly writing—about it. She was in short smartly making
up what she had missed, and he could take such comfort from his own action
as he had been helped to by the rest of the facts, succinctly reported from
Paris on the very morning of his start.

It was the singular story of a sharp split—in a good English house—
that dated now from years back. A worthy Briton, of the best middling
stock, had, during the fourth decade of the century, as a very young man, in
Dresden, whither he had been despatched to qualify in German for a stool
in an uncle's counting-house, met, admired, wooed and won an American
girl, of due attractions, domiciled at that period with her parents and a sister,
who was also attractive, in the Saxon capital. He had married her, taken her
to England, and there, after some years of harmony and happiness, lost her.
The sister in question had, after her death, come to him and to his young
child on a visit, the effect of which, between the pair, eventually defined itself
as a sentiment that was not to be resisted. The bereaved husband, yielding
to a new attachment and a new response, and finding a new union thus
prescribed, had yet been forced to reckon with the unaccommodating law of
the land. Encompassed with frowns in his own country, however, marriages
of this particular type were wreathed in smiles in his sister's-in-law, so that

his remedy was not forbidden. Choosing between two allegiances he had let the one go that seemed the least close, and had in brief transplanted his possibilities to an easier air. The knot was tied for the couple in New York, where, to protect the legitimacy of such other children as might come to them, they settled and prospered. Children came, and one of the daughters, growing up and marrying in her turn, was, if Frank rightly followed, the mother of his own Addie, who had been deprived of the knowledge of her indeed, in childhood, by death, and been brought up, though without undue tension, by a stepmother—a character breaking out thus anew.

The breach produced in England by the invidious action, as it was there held, of the girl's grandfather, had not failed to widen—all the more that nothing had been done on the American side to close it. Frigidity had settled, and hostility had been arrested only by indifference. Darkness therefore had fortunately supervened, and a cousinship completely divided. On either side of the impassable gulf, of the impenetrable curtain, each branch had put forth its leaves—a foliage wanting, in the American quarter, it was distinct enough to Granger, of no sign or symptom of climate and environment. The graft in New York had taken, and Addie was a vivid, an unmistakable flower. At Flickerbridge, or wherever, on the other hand, strange to say, the parent stem had had a fortune comparatively meagre. Fortune, it was true, in the vulgarest sense, had attended neither party. Addie's immediate belongings were as poor as they were numerous, and he gathered that Miss Wenham's pretensions to wealth were not so marked as to expose the claim of kinship to the imputation of motive. To this lady's single identity the original stock had at all events dwindled, and our young man was properly warned that he would find her shy and solitary. What was singular was that in these conditions she should desire, she should endure, to receive him. But that was all another story, lucid enough when mastered. He kept Addie's letters, exceptionally copious, in his lap; he conned them at intervals; he held the threads.

He looked out between whiles at the pleasant English land, an April *aquarelle* washed in with wondrous breadth. He knew the French thing, he knew the American, but he had known nothing of this. He saw it already as the remarkable Miss Wenham's setting. The doctor's daughter at Flickerbridge, with nippers on her nose, a palette on her thumb and innocence in her heart, had been the miraculous link. She had become aware even there, in our world of wonders, that the current fashion for young women so equipped was to enter the Parisian lists. Addie had accordingly chanced upon her, on the slopes of Montparnasse, as one of the English girls in one of the thorough-going sets. They had met in some easy collocation and had fallen upon common ground; after which the young woman, restored to Flickerbridge for an interlude and retailing there her adventures and impressions, had mentioned to Miss Wenham, who had known and protected her from babyhood, that that lady's own name of Adelaide was, as well as the surname conjoined with it, borne, to her knowledge, in Paris, by an extraordinary American specimen. She had then recrossed the Channel with a wonderful message, a courteous challenge, to her friend's duplicate, who had in turn granted through her every satisfaction. The duplicate had in other words bravely let Miss Wenham know exactly who she was. Miss Wenham, in whose personal tradition the flame of resentment appeared to have been reduced by time to the palest ashes—for whom indeed the story of the great schism was now but a legend only needing a little less dimness to make it romantic—Miss Wenham had promptly responded by a letter fragrant with the hope that old threads might be taken up. It was a relationship that they must puzzle out together, and she had earnestly sounded the other party to it on the subject of a possible visit. Addie had met her with a definite promise; she would come soon, she would come when free, she would come in July; but meanwhile she sent her deputy. Frank asked himself by what name she had described, by what character introduced him to Flickerbridge. He mainly felt on the whole as if he were going there to find out if he were engaged to her. He was at sea really now as to which of the various views Addie herself took of it. To Miss Wenham she must definitely have taken one, and perhaps Miss Wenham would reveal it. This expectation was in fact his excuse for a possible indiscretion.

CHAPTER III

He was indeed to learn on arrival to what he had been committed; but that was for a while so much a part of his first general impression that the particular truth took time to detach itself, the first general impression demanding verily all his faculties of response. He almost felt for a day or two the victim of a practical joke, a gross abuse of confidence. He had presented himself with the moderate amount of flutter involved in a sense of due preparation; but he had then found that, however primed with prefaces and prompted with hints, he hadn't been prepared at all. How *could* he be, he asked himself, for anything so foreign to his experience, so alien to his proper world, so little to be preconceived in the sharp north light of the newest impressionism, and yet so recognised after all in the event, so noted and tasted and assimilated? It was a case he would scarce have known how to describe— could doubtless have described best with a full clean brush, supplemented by a play of gesture; for it was always his habit to see an occasion, of whatever kind, primarily as a picture, so that he might get it, as he was wont to say, so that he might keep it, well together. He had been treated of a sudden, in this adventure, to one of the sweetest fairest coolest impressions of his life—one moreover visibly complete and homogeneous from the start. Oh it was *there*, if that was all one wanted of a thing! It was so "there" that, as had befallen him in Italy, in Spain, confronted at last, in dusky side-chapel or rich museum, with great things dreamed of or with greater ones unexpectedly presented, he had held his breath for fear of breaking the spell; had almost, from the quick impulse to respect, to prolong, lowered his voice and moved on tiptoe. Supreme beauty suddenly revealed is apt to strike us as a possible illusion playing with our desire—instant freedom with it to strike us as a possible rashness.

This fortunately, however—and the more so as his freedom for the time quite left him—didn't prevent his hostess, the evening of his advent and while the vision was new, from being exactly as queer and rare and *impayable*, as improbable, as impossible, as delightful at the eight o'clock dinner—she appeared to keep these immense hours—as she had overwhelmingly been at the five o'clock tea. She was in the most natural way in the world one of the oddest apparitions, but that the particular means to such an end *could* be natural was an inference difficult to make. He failed in fact to make it for a couple of days; but then—though then only—he made it with confidence. By this time indeed he was sure of everything, luckily including himself. If we compare his impression, with slight extravagance, to some of the greatest he had ever received, this is simply because the image before him was so rounded and stamped. It expressed with pure perfection, it exhausted its character. It was so absolutely and so unconsciously what it was. He had been floated by the strangest of chances out of the rushing stream into a clear still backwater—a deep and quiet pool in which objects were sharply mirrored. He had hitherto in life known nothing that was old except a few statues and pictures; but here everything was old, was immemorial, and nothing so much so as the very freshness itself. Vaguely to have supposed there were such nooks in the world had done little enough, he now saw, to temper the glare of their opposites. It was the fine touches that counted, and these had to be seen to be believed.

Miss Wenham, fifty-five years of age and unappeasably timid, unaccountably strange, had, on her reduced scale, an almost Gothic grotesqueness; but the final effect of one's sense of it was an amenity that accompanied one's steps like wafted gratitude. More flurried, more spasmodic, more apologetic, more completely at a loss at one moment and more precipitately abounding at another, he had never before in all his days seen any maiden lady; yet for no maiden lady he had ever seen had he so promptly conceived a private enthusiasm. Her eyes protruded, her chin receded and her nose carried on in conversation a queer little independent motion. She wore on the top of her head an upright circular cap that made her resemble a caryatid disburdened, and on other parts of her person strange combinations of colours, stuffs, shapes, of metal, mineral and plant. The tones of her voice rose and fell, her facial convulsions, whether tending—one could scarce make out—to expression or *re*pression, succeeded each other by a law of their own; she was embarrassed at nothing and at everything, frightened at everything and at nothing, and she approached objects, subjects, the simplest questions and answers and the whole material of intercourse, either with the indirectness of terror or with the violence of despair. These things, none the less, her refinements of oddity and intensities of custom, her betrayal at once of conventions and simplicities, of ease and of agony, her roundabout retarded suggestions and perceptions, still permitted her to strike her guest as irresistibly charming. He didn't know what to call it; she was a fruit of time. She had a queer distinction. She had been expensively produced and there would be a good deal more of her to come.

The result of the whole quality of her welcome, at any rate, was that the first evening, in his room, before going to bed, he relieved his mind in a letter to Addie, which, if space allowed us to embody it in our text, would usefully perform the office of a "plate." It would enable us to present ourselves as profusely illustrated. But the process of reproduction, as we say, costs. He wished his friend to know how grandly their affair turned out. She had put him in the way of something absolutely special—an old house untouched, untouchable, indescribable, an old corner such as one didn't believe existed, and the holy calm of which made the chatter of studios, the smell of paint, the slang of critics, the whole sense and sound of Paris, come back as so many signs of a huge monkey-cage. He moved about, restless, while he wrote; he lighted cigarettes and, nervous and suddenly scrupulous, put them out again; the night was mild and one of the windows of his large high room, which stood over the garden, was up. He lost himself in the things about him, in the type of the room, the last century with not a chair moved, not a point stretched. He hung over the objects and ornaments, blissfully few and adorably good, perfect pieces all, and never one, for a change, French. The scene was as rare as some fine old print with the best bits down in the corners. Old books and old pictures, allusions remembered and aspects conjectured, reappeared to him; he knew not what anxious islanders had been trying for in their backward hunt for the homely. But the homely at Flickerbridge was all style, even as style at the same time was mere honesty. The larger, the smaller past—he scarce knew which to call it—was at all events so hushed to sleep round him as he wrote that he had almost a bad conscience about having come. How one might love it, but how one might spoil it! To look at it too hard was positively to make it conscious, and to make it conscious was positively to wake it up. Its only safety, of a truth, was to be left still to sleep—to sleep in its large fair chambers and under its high clean canopies.

He added thus restlessly a line to his letter, maundered round the room again, noted and fingered something else, and then, dropping on the old flowered sofa, sustained by the tight cubes of its cushions, yielded afresh to the cigarette, hesitated, stared, wrote a few words more. He wanted Addie to know, that was what he most felt, unless he perhaps felt, more how much she herself would want to. Yes, what he supremely saw was all that Addie would make of it. Up to his neck in it there he fairly turned cold at the sense of suppressed opportunity, of the outrage of privation that his correspondent would retrospectively and, as he even divined with a vague shudder, almost vindictively nurse. Well, what had happened was that the acquaintance had been kept for her, like a packet enveloped and sealed for delivery, till her attention was free. He saw her there, heard her and felt her—felt how she would feel and how she would, as she usually said, "rave." Some of her young compatriots called it "yell," and in the reference itself, alas! illustrated their meaning. She would understand the place at any rate, down to the ground; there wasn't the slightest doubt of that. Her sense of it would be exactly like his own, and he could see, in anticipation, just the terms of recognition and rapture in which she would abound. He knew just what she would call quaint, just what she would call bland, just what she would call weird, just what she would call wild. She would take it all in with an intelligence much more fitted than his own, in fact, to deal with what he supposed he must regard as its literary relations. She would have read the long-winded obsolete memoirs and novels that both the figures and the setting ought clearly to remind one of; she would know about the past generations—the lumbering country magnates and their turbaned wives and round-eyed daughters, who, in other days, had treated the ruddy sturdy tradeless town,—the solid square houses and wide walled gardens, the streets to-day all grass and gossip, as the scene of a local "season." She would have warrant for the assemblies, dinners, deep potations; for the smoked sconces in the dusky parlours; for the long muddy century of family coaches, "holsters," highwaymen. She would put a finger in short, just as he had done, on the vital spot—the rich humility of the whole thing, the fact that neither Flickerbridge in general nor Miss Wenham in particular, nor anything nor any one concerned, had a suspicion of their characters and their merit. Addie and he would have to come to let in light.

He let it in then, little by little, before going to bed, through the eight or ten pages he addressed to her; assured her that it was the happiest case in the world, a little picture—yet full of "style" too—absolutely composed and transmitted, with tradition, and tradition only, in every stroke, tradition still noiselessly breathing and visibly flushing, marking strange hours in the tall mahogany clocks that were never wound up and that yet audibly ticked on. All the elements, he was sure he should see, would hang together with a charm, presenting his hostess—a strange iridescent fish for the glazed exposure of an aquarium—as afloat in her native medium. He left his letter open on the table, but, looking it over next morning, felt of a sudden indisposed to send it. He would keep it to add more, for there would be more to know; yet when three days had elapsed he still had not sent it. He sent instead, after delay, a much briefer report, which he was moved to make different and, for some reason, less vivid. Meanwhile he learned from Miss Wenham how Addie had introduced him. It took time to arrive with her at that point, but after the Rubicon was crossed they went far afield.

CHAPTER IV

"Oh yes, she said you were engaged to her. That was why—since I *had* broken out—she thought I might like to see you; as I assure you I've been so delighted to. But *aren't* you?" the good lady asked as if she saw in his face some ground for doubt.

"Assuredly—if she says so. It may seem very odd to you, but I haven't known, and yet I've felt that, being nothing whatever to you directly, I need some warrant for consenting thus to be thrust on you. We *were*," the young man explained, "engaged a year ago; but since then (if you don't mind my telling you such things; I feel now as if I could tell you anything!) I haven't quite known how I stand. It hasn't seemed we were in a position to marry. Things are better now, but I haven't quite known how she'd see them. They were so bad six months ago that I understood her, I thought, as breaking off. I haven't broken; I've only accepted, for the time—because men must be easy with women—being treated as 'the best of friends.' Well, I try to be. I wouldn't have come here if I hadn't been. I thought it would be charming for her to know you—when I heard from her the extraordinary way you had dawned upon her; and charming therefore if I could help her to it. And if I'm helping you to know *her*," he went on, "isn't that charming too?"

"Oh I so want to!" Miss Wenham murmured in her unpractical impersonal way. "You're so different!" she wistfully declared.

"It's *you*, if I may respectfully, ecstatically say so, who are different. That's the point of it all. I'm not sure that anything so terrible really ought to happen to you as to know us."

"Well," said Miss Wenham, "I do know you a little by this time, don't I? And I don't find it terrible. It's a delightful change for me."

"Oh I'm not sure you ought to have a delightful change!"

"Why not—if you do?"

"Ah I can bear it. I'm not sure you can. I'm too bad to spoil—I AM spoiled. I'm nobody, in short; I'm nothing. I've no type. You're *all* type. It has taken delicious long years of security and monotony to produce you. You fit your frame with a perfection only equalled by the perfection with which your frame fits you. So this admirable old house, all time-softened white within and time-faded red without, so everything that surrounds you here and that has, by some extraordinary mercy, escaped the inevitable fate of exploitation: so it all, I say, is the sort of thing that, were it the least bit to fall to pieces, could never, ah never more be put together again. I have, dear Miss Wenham," Granger went on, happy himself in his extravagance, which was yet all sincere, and happier still in her deep but altogether pleased mystification—"I've found, do you know, just the thing one has ever heard of that you most resemble. You're the Sleeping Beauty in the Wood."

He still had no compunction when he heard her bewilderedly sigh: "Oh you're too delightfully droll!"

"No, I only put thing's just as they are, and as I've also learned a little, thank heaven, to see them—which isn't, I quite agree with you, at all what any one does. You're in the deep doze of the spell that has held you for long years, and it would be a shame, a crime, to wake you up. Indeed I already feel with a thousand scruples that I'm giving you the fatal shake. I say it even though it makes me sound a little as if I thought myself the fairy prince."

She gazed at him with her queerest kindest look, which he was getting used to in spite of a faint fear, at the back of his head, of the strange things that sometimes occurred when lonely ladies, however mature, began to look at interesting young men from over the seas as if the young men desired to flirt. "It's so wonderful," she said, "that you should be so very odd and yet so very good-natured." Well, it all came to the same thing—it was so wonderful that *she* should be so simple and yet so little of a bore. He accepted with gratitude the theory of his languor—which moreover was real enough and partly perhaps why he was so sensitive; he let himself go as a convalescent, let her insist on the weakness always left by fever. It helped him to gain time, to preserve the spell even while he talked of breaking it; saw him through slow strolls and soft sessions, long gossips, fitful hopeless questions—there was so much more to tell than, by any contortion, she *could*—and explanations addressed gallantly and patiently to her understanding, but not, by good fortune, really reaching it. They were perfectly at cross-purposes, and it was the better, and they wandered together in the silver haze with all communication blurred.

When they sat in the sun in her formal garden he quite knew how little even the tenderest consideration failed to disguise his treating her as the most exquisite of curiosities. The term of comparison most present to him was that of some obsolete musical instrument. The old-time order of her mind and her air had the stillness of a painted spinnet that was duly dusted, gently rubbed, but never tuned nor played on. Her opinions were like dried rose-leaves; her attitudes like British sculpture; her voice what he imagined of the possible tone of the old gilded silver-stringed harp in one of the corners of the drawing-room. The lonely little decencies and modest dignities of her life, the fine grain of its conservatism, the innocence of its ignorance, all its monotony of stupidity and salubrity, its cold dulness and dim brightness, were there before him. Meanwhile within him strange things took place. It was literally true that his impression began again, after a lull, to make him nervous and anxious, and for reasons peculiarly confused, almost grotesquely mingled, or at least comically sharp. He was distinctly an agitation and a new taste—that he could see; and he saw quite as much therefore the excitement she already drew from the vision of Addie, an image intensified by the sense of closer kinship and presented to her, clearly, with various erratic enhancements, by her friend the doctor's daughter. At the end of a few days he said to her: "Do you know she wants to come without waiting any longer? She wants to come while I'm here. I received this morning her letter proposing it, but I've been thinking it over and have waited to speak to you. The thing is, you see, that if she writes to *you* proposing it—"

"Oh I shall be so particularly glad!"

CHAPTER V

They were as usual in the garden, and it hadn't yet been so present to him that if he were only a happy cad there would be a good way to protect her. As she wouldn't hear of his being yet beyond precautions she had gone into the house for a particular shawl that was just the thing for his knees, and, blinking in the watery sunshine, had come back with it across the fine little lawn. He was neither fatuous nor asinine, but he had almost to put it to himself as a small task to resist the sense of his absurd advantage with her. It filled him with horror and awkwardness, made him think of he didn't know what, recalled something of Maupassant's—the smitten "Miss Harriet" and her tragic fate. There was a preposterous possibility—yes, he held the strings quite in his hands—of keeping the treasure for himself. That was the art of life—what the real artist would consistently do. He would close the door on his impression, treat it as a private museum. He would see that he could lounge and linger there, live with wonderful things there, lie up there to rest and refit. For himself he was sure that after a little he should be able to paint there—do things in a key he had never thought of before. When she brought him the rug he took it from her and made her sit down on the bench and resume her knitting; then, passing behind her with a laugh, he placed it over her own shoulders; after which he moved to and fro before her, his hands in his pockets and his cigarette in his teeth. He was ashamed of the cigarette—a villainous false note; but she allowed, liked, begged him to smoke, and what he said to her on it, in one of the pleasantries she benevolently missed, was that he did so for fear of doing worse. That only showed how the end was really in sight. "I dare say it will strike you as quite awful, what I'm going to say to you, but I can't help it. I speak out of the depths of my respect for you. It will seem to you horrid disloyalty to poor Addie. Yes—there we are; there *I* am at least in my naked monstrosity." He stopped and looked at her till she might have been almost frightened. "Don't let her come. Tell her not to. I've tried to prevent it, but she suspects."

The poor woman wondered. "Suspects?"

"Well, I drew it, in writing to her, on reflexion, as mild as I could—having been visited in the watches of the night by the instinct of what might happen. Something told me to keep back my first letter—in which, under the first impression, I myself rashly 'raved'; and I concocted instead of it an insincere and guarded report. But guarded as I was I clearly didn't keep you 'down,' as we say, enough. The wonder of your colour—daub you over with grey as I might—must have come through and told the tale. She scents battle from afar—by which I mean she scents 'quaintness.' But keep her off. It's hideous, what I'm saying—but I owe it to you. I owe it to the world. She'll kill you."

"You mean I shan't get on with her?"

"Oh fatally! See how *I* have. And see how you have with ME. She's intelligent, moreover, remarkably pretty, remarkably good. And she'll adore you."

"Well then?"

"Why that will be just how she'll do for you."

"Oh I can hold my own!" said Miss Wenham with the headshake of a horse making his sleigh-bells rattle in frosty air.

"Ah but you can't hold hers! She'll rave about you. She'll write about you. You're Niagara before the first white traveller—and you know, or rather you can't know, what Niagara became *after* that gentleman. Addie will have discovered Niagara. She'll understand you in perfection; she'll feel you down to the ground; not a delicate shade of you will she lose or let any one else lose. You'll be too weird for words, but the words will nevertheless come. You'll be too exactly the real thing and be left too utterly just as you are, and all Addie's friends and all Addie's editors and contributors and readers will cross the Atlantic and flock to Flickerbridge just in order so—unanimously, universally, vociferously—to leave you. You'll be in the magazines with illustrations; you'll be in the papers with headings; you'll be everywhere with everything. You don't understand—you think you do, but you don't. Heaven forbid you *should* understand! That's just your beauty—your 'sleeping' beauty.

But you needn't. You can take me on trust. Don't have her. Give as a pretext, as a reason, anything in the world you like. Lie to her—scare her away. I'll go away and give you up—I'll sacrifice everything myself." Granger pursued his exhortation, convincing himself more and more. "If I saw my way out, my way completely through, I'D pile up some fabric of fiction for her—I should only want to be sure of its not tumbling down. One would have, you see, to keep the thing up. But I'd throw dust in her eyes. I'd tell her you don't do at all—that you're not in fact a desirable acquaintance. I'd tell her you're vulgar, improper, scandalous; I'd tell her you're mercenary, designing, dangerous; I'd tell her the only safe course is immediately to let you drop. I'd thus surround you with an impenetrable legend of conscientious misrepresentation, a circle of pious fraud, and all the while privately keep you for myself."

She had listened to him as if he were a band of music and she herself a small shy garden-party. "I shouldn't like you to go away. I shouldn't in the least like you not to come again."

"Ah there it is!" he replied. "How can I come again if Addie ruins you?"

"But how will she ruin me—even if she does what you say? I know I'm too old to change and really much too queer to please in any of the extraordinary ways you speak of. If it's a question of quizzing me I don't think my cousin, or any one else, will have quite the hand for it that *you* seem to have. So that if *you* haven't ruined me—!"

"But I *have*—that's just the point!" Granger insisted. "I've undermined you at least. I've left after all terribly little for Addie to do."

She laughed in clear tones. "Well then, we'll admit that you've done everything but frighten me."

He looked at her with surpassing gloom. "No—that again is one of the most dreadful features. You'll positively like it—what's to come. You'll be caught up in a chariot of fire like the prophet—wasn't there, was there one?— of old. That's exactly why—if one could but have done it—you'd have been to be kept ignorant and helpless. There's something or other in Latin that says it's the finest things that change the most easily for the worse. You already enjoy your dishonour and revel in your shame. It's too late—you're lost!"

CHAPTER VI

All this was as pleasant a manner of passing the time as any other, for it didn't prevent his old-world corner from closing round him more entirely, nor stand in the way of his making out from day to day some new source as well as some new effect of its virtue. He was really scared at moments at some of the liberties he took in talk—at finding himself so familiar; for the great note of the place was just that a certain modern ease had never crossed its threshold, that quick intimacies and quick oblivions were a stranger to its air. It had known in all its days no rude, no loud invasion. Serenely unconscious of most contemporary things, it had been so of nothing so much as of the diffused social practice of running in and out. Granger held his breath on occasions to think how Addie would run. There were moments when, more than at others, for some reason, he heard her step on the staircase and her cry in the hall. If he nevertheless played freely with the idea with which we have shown him as occupied it wasn't that in all palpable ways he didn't sacrifice so far as mortally possible to stillness. He only hovered, ever so lightly, to take up again his thread. She wouldn't hear of his leaving her, of his being in the least fit again, as she said, to travel. She spoke of the journey to London—which was in fact a matter of many hours—as an experiment fraught with lurking complications. He added then day to day, yet only hereby, as he reminded her, giving other complications a larger chance to multiply. He kept it before her, when there was nothing else to do, that she must consider; after which he had his times of fear that she perhaps really would make for him this sacrifice.

He knew she had written again to Paris, and knew he must himself again write—a situation abounding for each in the elements of a plight. If he stayed so long why then he wasn't better, and if he wasn't better Addie might take it into her head—! They must make it clear that he *was* better, so that, suspicious, alarmed at what was kept from her, she shouldn't suddenly present herself to nurse him. If he was better, however, why did he stay so long? If he stayed only for the attraction the sense of the attraction might be contagious. This was what finally grew clearest for him, so that he had for his mild disciple hours of still sharper prophecy. It consorted with his fancy to represent to her that their young friend had been by this time unsparingly warned; but nothing could be plainer than that this was ineffectual so long as he himself resisted the ordeal. To plead that he remained because he was too weak to move was only to throw themselves back on the other horn of their dilemma. If he was too weak to move Addie would bring him her strength—of which, when she got there, she would give them specimens enough. One morning he broke out at breakfast with an intimate conviction. They'd see that she was actually starting—they'd receive a wire by noon. They didn't receive it, but by his theory the portent was only the stronger. It had moreover its grave as well as its gay side, since Granger's paradox and pleasantry were only the method most open to him of conveying what he felt. He literally heard the knell sound, and in expressing this to Miss Wenham with the conversational freedom that seemed best to pay his way he the more vividly faced the contingency. He could never return, and though he announced it with a despair that did what might be to make it pass as a joke, he saw how, whether or no she at last understood, she quite at last believed him. On this, to his knowledge, she wrote again to Addie, and the contents of her letter excited his curiosity. But that sentiment, though not assuaged, quite dropped when, the day after, in the evening, she let him know she had had a telegram an hour before.

"She comes Thursday."

He showed not the least surprise. It was the deep calm of the fatalist. It *had* to be. "I must leave you then to-morrow."

She looked, on this, as he had never seen her; it would have been hard to say whether what showed in her face was the last failure to follow or the first effort to meet. "And really not to come back?"

"Never, never, dear lady. Why should I come back? You can never be again what you *have* been. I shall have seen the last of you."

"Oh!" she touchingly urged.

95

"Yes, for I should next find you simply brought to self-consciousness. You'll be exactly what you are, I charitably admit—nothing more or less, nothing different. But you'll be it all in a different way. We live in an age of prodigious machinery, all organised to a single end. That end is publicity—a publicity as ferocious as the appetite of a cannibal. The thing therefore is not to have any illusions—fondly to flatter yourself in a muddled moment that the cannibal will spare you. He spares nobody. He spares nothing. It will be all right. You'll have a lovely time. You'll be only just a public character—blown about the world 'for all you're worth,' and proclaimed 'for all you're worth' on the house-tops. It will be for *that*, mind, I quite recognise—because Addie is superior—as well as for all you aren't. So good-bye."

He remained however till the next day, and noted at intervals the different stages of their friend's journey; the hour, this time, she would really have started, the hour she'd reach Dover, the hour she'd get to town, where she'd alight at Mrs. Dunn's. Perhaps she'd bring Mrs. Dunn, for Mrs. Dunn would swell the chorus. At the last, on the morrow, as if in anticipation of this stillness settled between them: he became as silent as his hostess. But before he went she brought out shyly and anxiously, as an appeal, the question that for hours had clearly been giving her thought. "Do you meet her then to-night in London?"

"Dear no. In what position am I, alas! to do that? When can I *ever* meet her again?" He had turned it all over. "If I could meet Addie after this, you know, I could meet *you*. And if I do meet Addie," he lucidly pursued, "what will happen by the same stroke is that I *shall* meet you. And that's just what I've explained to you I dread."

"You mean she and I will be inseparable?"

He hesitated. "I mean she'll tell me all about you. I can hear her and her ravings now."

She gave again—and it was infinitely sad—her little whinnying laugh. "Oh but if what you say is true you'll know."

"Ah but Addie won't! Won't, I mean, know that *I* know—or at least won't believe it. Won't believe that any one knows. Such," he added with a strange smothered sigh, "is Addie. Do you know," he wound up, "that what, after all, has most definitely happened is that you've made me see her as I've never done before?"

She blinked and gasped, she wondered and despaired. "Oh no, it will be *you*. I've had nothing to do with it. Everything's all you!"

But for all it mattered now! "You'll see," he said, "that she's charming. I shall go for to-night to Oxford. I shall almost cross her on the way."

"Then if she's charming what am I to tell her from you in explanation of such strange behaviour as your flying away just as she arrives?"

"Ah you needn't mind about that—you needn't tell her anything."

She fixed him as if as never again. "It's none of my business, of course I feel; but isn't it a little cruel if you're engaged?"

Granger gave a laugh almost as odd as one of her own. "Oh you've cost me that!"—and he put out his hand to her.

She wondered while she took it. "Cost you—?"

"We're not engaged. Good-bye."

MRS. MEDWIN

CHAPTER I

"Well, we *are* a pair!" the poor lady's visitor broke out to her at the end of her explanation in a manner disconcerting enough. The poor lady was Miss Cutter, who lived in South Audley Street, where she had an "upper half" so concise that it had to pass boldly for convenient; and her visitor was her half-brother, whom she hadn't seen for three years. She was remarkable for a maturity of which every symptom might have been observed to be admirably controlled, had not a tendency to stoutness just affirmed its independence. Her present, no doubt, insisted too much on her past, but with the excuse, sufficiently valid, that she must certainly once have been prettier. She was clearly not contented with once—she wished to be prettier again. She neglected nothing that could produce that illusion, and, being both fair and fat, dressed almost wholly in black. When she added a little colour it was not, at any rate, to her drapery. Her small rooms had the peculiarity that everything they contained appeared to testify with vividness to her position in society, quite as if they had been furnished by the bounty of admiring friends. They were adorned indeed almost exclusively with objects that nobody buys, as had more than once been remarked by spectators of her own sex, for herself, and would have been luxurious if luxury consisted mainly in photographic portraits slashed across with signatures, in baskets of flowers beribboned with the cards of passing compatriots, and in a neat collection of red volumes, blue volumes, alphabetical volumes, aids to London lucidity, of every sort, devoted to addresses and engagements. To be in Miss Cutter's tiny drawing-room, in short, even with Miss Cutter alone—should you by any chance have found her so—was somehow to be in the world and in a crowd. It was like an agency—it bristled with particulars.

This was what the tall lean loose gentleman lounging there before her might have appeared to read in the suggestive scene over which, while she talked to him, his eyes moved without haste and without rest. "Oh come, Mamie!" he occasionally threw off; and the words were evidently connected with the impression thus absorbed. His comparative youth spoke of waste even as her positive—her too positive—spoke of economy. There was only one thing, that is, to make up in him for everything he had lost, though it was distinct enough indeed that this thing might sometimes serve. It consisted in the perfection of an indifference, an indifference at the present moment directed to the plea—a plea of inability, of pure destitution—with which his sister had met him. Yet it had even now a wider embrace, took in quite sufficiently all consequences of queerness, confessed in advance to the false note that, in such a setting, he almost excruciatingly constituted. He cared as little that he looked at moments all his impudence as that he looked all his shabbiness, all his cleverness, all his history. These different things were written in him—in his premature baldness, his seamed strained face, the lapse from bravery of his long tawny moustache; above all in his easy friendly universally acquainted eye, so much too sociable for mere conversation. What possible relation with him could be natural enough to meet it? He wore a scant rough Inverness cape and a pair of black trousers, wanting in substance and marked with the sheen of time, that had presumably once served for evening use. He spoke with the slowness helplessly permitted to Americans—as something too slow to be stopped—and he repeated that he found himself associated with Miss Cutter in a harmony calling for wonder. She had been telling him not only that she couldn't possibly give him ten pounds, but that his unexpected arrival, should he insist on being much in view, might seriously interfere with arrangements necessary to her own maintenance; on which he had begun by replying that he of course knew she had long ago spent her money, but that he looked to her now exactly because she had, without the aid of that convenience, mastered the art of life.

"I'd really go away with a fiver, my dear, if you'd only tell me how you do it. It's no use saying only, as you've always said, that 'people are very kind to you.' What the devil are they kind to you *for*?"

"Well, one reason is precisely that no particular inconvenience has hitherto been supposed to attach to me. I'm just what I am," said Mamie Cutter; "nothing less and nothing more. It's awkward to have to explain to you, which moreover I really needn't in the least. I'm clever and amusing and charming." She was uneasy and even frightened, but she kept her temper and met him with a grace of her own. "I don't think you ought to ask me more questions than I ask you."

"Ah my dear," said the odd young man, "I'VE no mysteries. Why in the world, since it was what you came out for and have devoted so much of your time to, haven't you pulled it off? Why haven't you married?"

"Why haven't *you*?" she retorted. "Do you think that if I had it would have been better for you?—that my husband would for a moment have put up with you? Do you mind my asking you if you'll kindly go *now*?" she went on after a glance at the clock. "I'm expecting a friend, whom I must see alone, on a matter of great importance—"

"And my being seen with you may compromise your respectability or undermine your nerve?" He sprawled imperturbably in his place, crossing again, in another sense, his long black legs and showing, above his low shoes, an absurd reach of parti-coloured sock. "I take your point well enough, but mayn't you be after all quite wrong? If you can't do anything for me couldn't you at least do something with me? If it comes to that, I'm clever and amusing and charming too! I've been such an ass that you don't appreciate me. But people like me—I assure you they do. They usually don't know what an ass I've been; they only see the surface, which"—and he stretched himself afresh as she looked him up and down—"you *can* imagine them, can't you, rather taken with? I'M 'what I am' too; nothing less and nothing more. That's true of us as a family, you see. We *are* a crew!" He delivered himself serenely. His voice was soft and flat, his pleasant eyes, his simple tones tending to the solemn, achieved at moments that effect of quaintness which is, in certain connexions, socially so known and enjoyed. "English people have quite a weakness for me—more than any others. I get on with them beautifully. I've always been with them abroad. They think me," the young man explained, "diabolically American."

"You!" Such stupidity drew from her a sigh of compassion.

Her companion apparently quite understood it. "Are you homesick, Mamie?" he asked, with wondering irrelevance.

The manner of the question made her, for some reason, in spite of her preoccupations, break into a laugh. A shade of indulgence, a sense of other things, came back to her. "You are funny, Scott!"

"Well," remarked Scott, "that's just what I claim. But *are* you so homesick?" he spaciously inquired, not as to a practical end, but from an easy play of intelligence.

"I'm just dying of it!" said Mamie Cutter.

"Why so am I!" Her visitor had a sweetness of concurrence.

"We're the only decent people," Miss Cutter declared. "And I know. You don't—you can't; and I can't explain. Come in," she continued with a return of her impatience and an increase of her decision, "at seven sharp."

She had quitted her seat some time before, and now, to get him into motion, hovered before him while, still motionless, he looked up at her. Something intimate, in the silence, appeared to pass between them—a community of fatigue and failure and, after all, of intelligence. There was a final cynical humour in it. It determined him, in any case, at last, and he slowly rose, taking in again as he stood there the testimony of the room. He might have been counting the photographs, but he looked at the flowers with detachment. "Who's coming?"

"Mrs. Medwin."

"American?"

"Dear no!"

"Then what are you doing for her?"

"I work for every one," she promptly returned.

"For every one who pays? So I suppose. Yet isn't it only we who do pay?"

There was a drollery, not lost on her, in the way his queer presence lent itself to his emphasised plural.

"Do you consider that *you* do?"

At this, with his deliberation, he came back to his charming idea. "Only try me, and see if I can't be *made* to. Work me in." On her sharply presenting her back he stared a little at the clock. "If I come at seven may I stay to dinner?"

It brought her round again. "Impossible. I'm dining out."

"With whom?"

She had to think. "With Lord Considine."

"Oh my eye!" Scott exclaimed.

She looked at him gloomily. "Is *that* sort of tone what makes you pay? I think you might understand," she went on, "that if you're to sponge on me successfully you mustn't ruin me. I must have *some* remote resemblance to a lady."

"Yes? But why must *I*?" Her exasperated silence was full of answers, of which however his inimitable manner took no account. "You don't understand my real strength; I doubt if you even understand your own. You're clever, Mamie, but you're not so clever as I supposed. However," he pursued, "it's out of Mrs. Medwin that you'll get it."

"Get what?"

"Why the cheque that will enable you to assist me."

On this, for a moment, she met his eyes. "If you'll come back at seven sharp—not a minute before, and not a minute after, I'll give you two five-pound notes."

He thought it over. "Whom are you expecting a minute after?"

It sent her to the window with a groan almost of anguish, and she answered nothing till she had looked at the street. "If you injure me, you know, Scott, you'll be sorry."

"I wouldn't injure you for the world. What I want to do in fact is really to help you, and I promise you that I won't leave you—by which I mean won't leave London—till I've effected something really pleasant for you. I like you, Mamie, because I like pluck; I like you much more than you like me. I like you very, *very* much." He had at last with this reached the door and opened it, but he remained with his hand on the latch. "What does Mrs. Medwin want of you?" he thus brought out.

She had come round to see him disappear, and in the relief of this prospect she again just indulged him.

"The impossible."

He waited another minute. "And you're going to do it?"

"I'm going to do it," said Mamie Cutter.

"Well then that ought to be a haul. Call it *three* fivers!" he laughed. "At seven sharp." And at last he left her alone.

CHAPTER II

Miss Cutter waited till she heard the house-door close; after which, in a sightless mechanical way, she moved about the room readjusting various objects he had not touched. It was as if his mere voice and accent had spoiled her form. But she was not left too long to reckon with these things, for Mrs. Medwin was promptly announced. This lady was not, more than her hostess, in the first flush of her youth; her appearance—the scattered remains of beauty manipulated by taste—resembled one of the light repasts in which the fragments of yesterday's dinner figure with a conscious ease that makes up for the want of presence. She was perhaps of an effect still too immediate to be called interesting, but she was candid, gentle and surprised—not fatiguingly surprised, only just in the right degree; and her white face—it was too white—with the fixed eyes, the somewhat touzled hair and the Louis Seize hat, might at the end of the very long neck have suggested the head of a princess carried on a pike in a revolution. She immediately took up the business that had brought her, with the air however of drawing from the omens then discernible less confidence than she had hoped. The complication lay in the fact that if it was Mamie's part to present the omens, that lady yet had so to colour them as to make her own service large. She perhaps over-coloured; for her friend gave way to momentary despair.

"What you mean is then that it's simply impossible?"

"Oh no," said Mamie with a qualified emphasis. "It's *possible*."

"But disgustingly difficult?"

"As difficult as you like."

"Then what can I do that I haven't done?"

"You can only wait a little longer."

"But that's just what I *have* done. I've done nothing else. I'm always waiting a little longer!"

Miss Cutter retained, in spite of this pathos, her grasp of the subject. "*The* thing, as I've told you, is for you first to be seen."

"But if people won't look at me?"

"They will."

"They *will*?" Mrs. Medwin was eager.

"They shall," her hostess went on. "It's their only having heard—without having seen.'"

"But if they stare straight the other way?" Mrs. Medwin continued to object. "You can't simply go up to them and twist their heads about."

"It's just what I can," said Mamie Cutter.

But her charming visitor, heedless for the moment of this attenuation, had found the way to put it. "It's the old story. You can't go into the water till you swim, and you can't swim till you go into the water. I can't be spoken to till I'm seen, but I can't be seen till I'm spoken to."

She met this lucidity, Miss Cutter, with but an instant's lapse. "You say I can't twist their heads about. But I *have* twisted them."

It had been quietly produced, but it gave her companion a jerk. "They say 'Yes'?"

She summed it up. "All but one. *She* says 'No.'"

Mrs. Medwin thought; then jumped. "Lady Wantridge?"

Miss Cutter, as more delicate, only bowed admission. "I shall see her either this afternoon or late to-morrow. But she has written."

Her visitor wondered again. "May I see her letter?"

"No." She spoke with decision. "But I shall square her."

"Then how?"

"Well"—and Miss Cutter, as if looking upward for inspiration, fixed her eyes a while on the ceiling—"well, it will come to me."

Mrs. Medwin watched her—it was impressive. "And will they come to you—the others?" This question drew out the fact that they would—so far at least as they consisted of Lady Edward, Lady Bellhouse and Mrs. Pouncer, who had engaged to muster, at the signal of tea, on the 14th—prepared, as it were, for the worst. There was of course always the chance that Lady Wantridge might take the field, in such force as to paralyse them, though that danger, at the same time, seemed inconsistent with her being squared. It didn't perhaps all quite ideally hang together; but what it sufficiently came to was that if she was the one who could do most *for* a person in Mrs. Medwin's position she was also the one who could do most against. It would therefore be distinctly what our friend familiarly spoke of as "collar-work." The effect of these mixed considerations was at any rate that Mamie eventually acquiesced in the idea, handsomely thrown out by her client, that she should have an "advance" to go on with. Miss Cutter confessed that it seemed at times as if one scarce *could* go on; but the advance was, in spite of this delicacy, still more delicately made—made in the form of a banknote, several sovereigns, some loose silver, and two coppers, the whole contents of her purse, neatly disposed by Mrs. Medwin on one of the tiny tables. It seemed to clear the air for deeper intimacies, the fruit of which was that Mamie, lonely after all in her crowd and always more helpful than helped, eventually brought out that the way Scott had been going on was what seemed momentarily to overshadow her own power to do so.

"I've had a descent from him." But she had to explain. "My half-brother—Scott Homer. A wretch."

"What kind of a wretch?"

"Every kind. I lose sight of him at times—he disappears abroad. But he always turns up again, worse than ever."

"Violent?"

"No."

"Maudlin?"

"No."

"Only unpleasant?"

"No. Rather pleasant. Awfully clever—awfully travelled and easy."

"Then what's the matter with him?"

Mamie mused, hesitated—seemed to see a wide past. "I don't know."

"Something in the background?" Then as her friend was silent, "Something queer about cards?" Mrs. Medwin threw off.

"I don't know—and I don't want to!"

"Ah well, I'm sure *I* don't," Mrs. Medwin returned with spirit. The note of sharpness was perhaps also a little in the observation she made as she gathered herself to go. "Do you mind my saying something?"

Mamie took her eyes quickly from the money on the little stand. "You may say what you like."

"I only mean that anything awkward you may have to keep out of the way does seem to make more wonderful, doesn't it, that you should have got just where you are? I allude, you know, to your position."

"I see." Miss Cutter somewhat coldly smiled. "To my power."

"So awfully remarkable in an American."

"Ah you like us so."

Mrs. Medwin candidly considered. "But we don't, dearest."

Her companion's smile brightened. "Then why do you come to me?"

"Oh I like *you*!" Mrs. Medwin made out.

"Then that's it. There are no 'Americans.' It's always 'you.'"

"Me?" Mrs. Medwin looked lovely, but a little muddled.

"ME!" Mamie Cutter laughed. "But if you like me, you dear thing, you can judge if I like *you*." She gave her a kiss to dismiss her. "I'll see you again when I've seen her."

"Lady Wantridge? I hope so, indeed. I'll turn up late to-morrow, if you don't catch me first. Has it come to you yet?" the visitor, now at the door, went on.

"No; but it will. There's time."

"Oh a little less every day!"

Miss Cutter had approached the table and glanced again at the gold and silver and the note, not indeed absolutely overlooking the two coppers. "The balance," she put it, "the day after?"

"That very night if you like."

"Then count on me."

"Oh if I didn't—!" But the door closed on the dark idea. Yearningly then, and only when it had done so, Miss Cutter took up the money.

She went out with it ten minutes later, and, the calls on her time being many, remained out so long that at half-past six she hadn't come back. At that hour, on the other hand, Scott Homer knocked at her door, where her maid, who opened it with a weak pretence of holding it firm, ventured to announce to him, as a lesson well learnt, that he hadn't been expected till seven. No lesson, none the less, could prevail against his native art. He pleaded fatigue, her, the maid's, dreadful depressing London, and the need to curl up somewhere. If she'd just leave him quiet half an hour that old sofa upstairs would do for it; of which he took quickly such effectual possession that when five minutes later she peeped, nervous for her broken vow, into the drawing-room, the faithless young woman found him extended at his length and peacefully asleep.

CHAPTER III

The situation before Miss Cutter's return developed in other directions still, and when that event took place, at a few minutes past seven, these circumstances were, by the foot of the stair, between mistress and maid, the subject of some interrogative gasps and scared admissions. Lady Wantridge had arrived shortly after the interloper, and wishing, as she said, to wait, had gone straight up in spite of being told he was lying down.

"She distinctly understood he was there?"

"Oh yes ma'am; I thought it right to mention."

"And what did you call him?"

"Well, ma'am, I thought it unfair to *you* to call him anything but a gentleman."

Mamie took it all in, though there might well be more of it than one could quickly embrace. "But if she has had time," she flashed, "to find out he isn't one?"

"Oh ma'am, she had a quarter of an hour."

"Then she isn't with him still?"

"No ma'am; she came down again at last. She rang, and I saw her here, and she said she wouldn't wait longer."

Miss Cutter darkly mused. "Yet had already waited—?"

"Quite a quarter."

"Mercy on us!" She began to mount. Before reaching the top however she had reflected that quite a quarter was long if Lady Wantridge had only been shocked. On the other hand it was short if she had only been pleased. But how *could* she have been pleased? The very essence of their actual crisis was just that there was no pleasing her. Mamie had but to open the drawing-room door indeed to perceive that this was not true at least of Scott Homer, who was horribly cheerful.

Miss Cutter expressed to her brother without reserve her sense of the constitutional, the brutal selfishness that had determined his mistimed return. It had taken place, in violation of their agreement, exactly at the moment when it was most cruel to her that he should be there, and if she must now completely wash her hands of him he had only himself to thank. She had come in flushed with resentment and for a moment had been voluble, but it would have been striking that, though the way he received her might have seemed but to aggravate, it presently justified him by causing their relation really to take a stride. He had the art of confounding those who would quarrel with him by reducing them to the humiliation of a stirred curiosity.

"What *could* she have made of you?" Mamie demanded.

"My dear girl, she's not a woman who's eager to make too much of anything—anything, I mean, that will prevent her from doing as she likes, what she takes into her head. Of course," he continued to explain, "if it's something she doesn't want to do, she'll make as much as Moses."

Mamie wondered if that was the way he talked to her visitor, but felt obliged to own to his acuteness. It was an exact description of Lady Wantridge, and she was conscious of tucking it away for future use in a corner of her miscellaneous little mind. She withheld however all present acknowledgment, only addressing him another question. "Did you really get on with her?"

"Have you still to learn, darling—I can't help again putting it to you—that I get on with everybody? That's just what I don't seem able to drive into you. Only see how I get on with *you*."

She almost stood corrected. "What I mean is of course whether—"

"Whether she made love to me? Shyly, yet—or because—shamefully? She would certainly have liked awfully to stay."

"Then why didn't she?"

"Because, on account of some other matter—and I could see it was true—she hadn't time. Twenty minutes—she was here less—were all she came to give you. So don't be afraid I've frightened her away. She'll come back."

Mamie thought it over. "Yet you didn't go with her to the door?"

"She wouldn't let me, and I know when to do what I'm told—quite as much as what I'm not told. She wanted to find out about me. I mean from your little creature; a pearl of fidelity, by the way."

"But what on earth did she come up for?" Mamie again found herself appealing, and just by that fact showing her need of help.

"Because she always goes up." Then as, in the presence of this rapid generalisation, to say nothing of that of such a relative altogether, Miss Cutter could only show as comparatively blank: "I mean she knows when to go up and when to come down. She has instincts; she didn't know whom you might have up here. It's a kind of compliment to you anyway. Why Mamie," Scott pursued, "you don't know the curiosity we any of us inspire. You wouldn't believe what I've seen. The bigger bugs they are the more they're on the lookout."

Mamie still followed, but at a distance. "The lookout for what?"

"Why for anything that will help them to live. You've been here all this time without making out then, about them, what I've had to pick out as I can? They're dead, don't you see? And WE'RE alive."

"You? Oh!"—Mamie almost laughed about it.

"Well, they're a worn-out old lot anyhow; they've used up their resources. They do look out and I'll do them the justice to say they're not afraid—not even of me!" he continued as his sister again showed something of the same irony. "Lady Wantridge at any rate wasn't; that's what I mean by her having made love to me. She does what she likes. Mind it, you know." He was by this time fairly teaching her to read one of her best friends, and when, after it, he had come back to the great point of his lesson—that of her failure, through feminine inferiority, practically to grasp the truth that their being just as they were, he and she, was the real card for them to play—when he had renewed that reminder he left her absolutely in a state of dependence. Her impulse to press him on the subject of Lady Wantridge dropped; it was as if she had felt that, whatever had taken place, something would somehow come of it. She was to be in a manner disappointed, but the impression helped to keep her over to the next morning, when, as Scott had foretold, his new acquaintance did reappear, explaining to Miss Cutter that she had acted the day before to gain time and that she even now sought to gain it by not waiting longer. What, she promptly intimated she had asked herself, could that friend be thinking of? She must show where she stood before things had gone too far. If she had brought her answer without more delay she wished to make it sharp. Mrs. Medwin? Never! "No, my dear—not I. *There* I stop."

Mamie had known it would be "collar-work," but somehow now, at the beginning she felt her heart sink. It was not that she had expected to carry the position with a rush, but that, as always after an interval, her visitor's defences really loomed—and quite, as it were, to the material vision—too large. She was always planted with them, voluminous, in the very centre of the passage; was like a person accommodated with a chair in some unlawful place at the theatre. She wouldn't move and you couldn't get round. Mamie's calculation indeed had not been on getting round; she was obliged to recognise that, too foolishly and fondly, she had dreamed of inducing a surrender. Her dream had been the fruit of her need; but, conscious that she was even yet unequipped for pressure, she felt, almost for the first time in her life, superficial and crude. She was to be paid—but with what was she, to that end, to pay? She had engaged to find an answer to this question, but the answer had not, according to her promise, "come." And Lady Wantridge meanwhile massed herself, and there was no view of her that didn't show her as verily, by some process too obscure to be traced, the hard depository of the social law. She was no younger, no fresher, no stronger, really, than any of them; she was only, with a kind of haggard fineness, a sharpened taste for life, and, with all sorts of things behind and beneath her, more abysmal and more immoral, more secure and more impertinent. The points she made were two in number. One was that she absolutely declined; the other was that she quite doubted if Mamie herself had measured the job. The thing couldn't be done. But say it *could* be; was

Mamie quite the person to do it? To this Miss Cutter, with a sweet smile, replied that she quite understood how little she might seem so. "I'm only one of the persons to whom it has appeared that *you* are."

"Then who are the others?"

"Well, to begin with, Lady Edward, Lady Bellhouse and Mrs. Pouncer."

"Do you mean that they'll come to meet her?"

"I've seen them, and they've promised."

"To come, of course," Lady Wantridge said, "if *I* come."

Her hostess cast about. "Oh of course you could prevent them. But I should take it as awfully kind of you not to. *Won'*T you do this for me?" Mamie pleaded.

Her friend looked over the room very much as Scott had done. "Do they really understand what it's *for?*"

"Perfectly. So that she may call."

"And what good will that do her?"

Miss Cutter faltered, but she presently brought it out. "Naturally what one hopes is that, you'll ask her."

"Ask her to call?"

"Ask her to dine. Ask her, if you'd be so truly sweet, for a Sunday; or something of that sort, and even if only in one of your *most* mixed parties, to Catchmore."

Miss Cutter felt the less hopeful after this effort in that her companion only showed a strange good nature. And it wasn't a satiric amiability, though it *was* amusement. "Take Mrs. Medwin into my family?"

"Some day when you're taking forty others."

"Ah but what I don't see is what it does for *you.* You're already so welcome among us that you can scarcely improve your position even by forming for us the most delightful relation."

"Well, I know how dear you are," Mamie Cutter replied; "but one has after all more than one side and more than one sympathy. I like her, you know." And even at this Lady Wantridge wasn't shocked; she showed that ease and blandness which were her way, unfortunately, of being most impossible. She remarked that *she* might listen to such things, because she was clever enough for them not to matter; only Mamie should take care how she went about saying them at large. When she became definite however, in a minute, on the subject of the public facts, Miss Cutter soon found herself ready to make her own concession. Of course she didn't dispute *them*: there they were; they were unfortunately on record, and, nothing was to be done about them but to—Mamie found it in truth at this point a little difficult.

"Well, what? Pretend already to have forgotten them?"

"Why not, when you've done it in so many other cases?"

"There *are* no other cases so bad. One meets them at any rate as they come. Some you can manage, others you can't. It's no use, you must give them up. They're past patching; there's nothing to be done with them. There's nothing accordingly to be done with Mrs. Medwin but to put her off." And Lady Wantridge rose to her height.

"Well, you know, I DO do things," Mamie quavered with a smile so strained that it partook of exaltation.

"You help people? Oh yes, I've known you to do wonders. But stick," said Lady Wantridge with strong and cheerful emphasis, "to your Americans!"

Miss Cutter, gazing, got up. "You don't do justice, Lady Wantridge, to your own compatriots. Some of them are really charming. Besides," said Mamie, "working for mine often strikes me, so far as the interest—the inspiration and excitement, don't you know?—go, as rather too easy. You all, as I constantly have occasion to say, like us so!"

Her companion frankly weighed it. "Yes; it takes that to account for your position. I've always thought of you nevertheless as keeping for their benefit a regular working agency. They come to you, and you place them. There remains, I confess," her ladyship went on in the same free spirit, "the great wonder—"

"Of how I first placed my poor little self? Yes," Mamie bravely conceded, "when *I* began there was no agency. I just worked my passage. I didn't even come to *you*, did I? You never noticed me till, as Mrs. Short Stokes says, 'I was 'way, 'way up!' Mrs. Medwin," she threw in, "can't get over it." Then, as her friend looked vague: "Over my social situation."

"Well, it's no great flattery to you to say," Lady Wantridge good-humouredly returned, "that she certainly can't hope for one resembling it." Yet it really seemed to spread there before them. "You simply *made* Mrs. Short Stokes."

"In spite of her name!" Mamie smiled.

"Oh your 'names'—! In spite of everything."

"Ah I'm something of an artist." With which, and a relapse marked by her wistful eyes into the gravity of the matter, she supremely fixed her friend. She felt how little she minded betraying at last the extremity of her need, and it was out of this extremity that her appeal proceeded. "Have I really had your last word? It means so much to me."

Lady Wantridge came straight to the point. "You mean you depend on it?"

"Awfully!"

"Is it all you have?"

"All. Now."

"But Mrs. Short Stokes and the others—'rolling,' aren't they? Don't they pay up?"

"Ah," sighed Mamie, "if it wasn't for *them*—!"

Lady Wantridge perceived. "You've had so much?"

"I couldn't have gone on."

"Then what do you do with it all?"

"Oh most of it goes back to them. There are all sorts, and it's all help. Some of them have nothing."

"Oh if you feed the hungry," Lady Wantridge laughed, "you're indeed in a great way of business. Is Mrs. Medwin"—her transition was immediate—"really rich?"

"Really. He left her everything."

"So that if I do say 'yes'—"

"It will quite set me up."

"I see—and how much more responsible it makes one! But I'd rather myself give you the money."

"Oh!" Mamie coldly murmured.

"You mean I mayn't suspect your prices? Well, I daresay I don't! But I'd rather give you ten pounds."

"Oh!" Mamie repeated in a tone that sufficiently covered her prices. The question was in every way larger. "Do you never forgive?" she reproachfully inquired. The door opened however at the moment she spoke and Scott Homer presented himself.

CHAPTER IV

Scott Homer wore exactly, to his sister's eyes, the aspect he had worn the day before, and it also formed to her sense the great feature of his impartial greeting.

"How d'ye do, Mamie? How d'ye do, Lady Wantridge?"

"How d'ye do again?" Lady Wantridge replied with an equanimity striking to her hostess. It was as if Scott's own had been contagious; it was almost indeed as if she had seen him before. Had she ever so seen him—before the previous day? While Miss Cutter put to herself this question her visitor at all events met the one she had previously uttered. "Ever 'forgive'?" this personage echoed in a tone that made as little account as possible of the interruption. "Dear yes! The people I *have* forgiven!" She laughed—perhaps a little nervously; and she was now looking at Scott. The way she looked at him was precisely what had already had its effect for his sister. "The people I can!"

"Can you forgive me?" asked Scott Homer.

She took it so easily. "But—what?"

Mamie interposed; she turned directly to her brother. "Don't try her. Leave it so." She had had an inspiration, it was the most extraordinary thing in the world. "Don't try *him*"—she had turned to their companion. She looked grave, sad, strange. "Leave it so." Yes, it was a distinct inspiration, which she couldn't have explained, but which had come, prompted by something she had caught—the extent of the recognition expressed—in Lady Wantridge's face. It had come absolutely of a sudden, straight out of the opposition of the two figures before her—quite as if a concussion had struck a light. The light was helped by her quickened sense that her friend's silence on the incident of the day before showed some sort of consciousness. She looked surprised. "Do you know my brother?"

"DO I know you?" Lady Wantridge asked of him.

"No, Lady Wantridge," Scott pleasantly confessed, "not one little mite!"

"Well then if you *must* go—" and Mamie offered her a hand. "But I'll go down with you. *Not you!*" she launched at her brother, who immediately effaced himself. His way of doing so—and he had already done so, as for Lady Wantridge, in respect to their previous encounter—struck her even at the moment as an instinctive if slightly blind tribute to her possession of an idea; and as such, in its celerity, made her so admire him, and their common wit, that she on the spot more than forgave him his queerness. He was right. He could be as queer as he liked! The queerer the better! It was at the foot of the stairs, when she had got her guest down, that what she had assured Mrs. Medwin would come did indeed come. "*Did* you meet him here yesterday?"

"Dear yes. Isn't he too funny?"

"Yes," said Mamie gloomily. "He IS funny. But had you ever met him before?"

"Dear no!"

"Oh!"—and Mamie's tone might have meant many things.

Lady Wantridge however, after all, easily overlooked it. "I only knew he was one of your odd Americans. That's why, when I heard yesterday here that he was up there awaiting your return, I didn't let that prevent me. I thought he might be. He certainly," her ladyship laughed, "IS."

"Yes, he's very American," Mamie went on in the same way.

"As you say, we *are* fond of you! Good-bye," said Lady Wantridge.

But Mamie had not half done with her. She felt more and more—or she hoped at least—that she looked strange. She *was*, no doubt, if it came to that, strange. "Lady Wantridge," she almost convulsively broke out, "I don't know whether you'll understand me, but I seem to feel that I must act with you—I don't know what to call it!—responsibly. He IS my brother."

"Surely—and why not?" Lady Wantridge stared. "He's the image of you!"

"Thank you!"—and Mamie was stranger than ever.

"Oh he's good-looking. He's handsome, my dear. Oddly—but distinctly!" Her ladyship was for treating it much as a joke.

But Mamie, all sombre, would have none of this. She boldly gave him up. "I think he's awful."

"He is indeed—delightfully. And where DO you get your ways of saying things? It isn't anything—and the things aren't anything. But it's so droll."

"Don't let yourself, all the same," Mamie consistently pursued, "be carried away by it. The thing can't be done—simply."

Lady Wantridge wondered. "'Done simply'?"

"Done at all."

"But what can't be?"

"Why, what you might think—from his pleasantness. What he spoke of your doing for him."

Lady Wantridge recalled. "Forgiving him?"

"He asked you if you couldn't. But you can't. It's too dreadful for me, as so near a relation, to have, loyally—loyally to *you*—to say it. But he's impossible."

It was so portentously produced that her ladyship had somehow to meet it. "What's the matter with him?"

"I don't know."

"Then what's the matter with *you*?" Lady Wantridge inquired.

"It's because I *won't* know," Mamie—not without dignity—explained.

"Then *I* won't either."

"Precisely. Don't. It's something," Mamie pursued, with some inconsequence, "that—somewhere or other, at some time or other—he appears to have done. Something that has made a difference in his life."

119

"'Something'?" Lady Wantridge echoed again. "What kind of thing?"

Mamie looked up at the light above the door, through which the London sky was doubly dim. "I haven't the least idea."

"Then what kind of difference?"

Mamie's gaze was still at the light. "The difference you see."

Lady Wantridge, rather obligingly, seemed to ask herself what she saw. "But I don't see any! It seems, at least," she added, "such an amusing one! And he has such nice eyes."

"Oh *dear* eyes!" Mamie conceded; but with too much sadness, for the moment, about the connexions of the subject, to say more.

It almost forced her companion after an instant to proceed. "Do you mean he can't go home?"

She weighed her responsibility. "I only make out—more's the pity!—that he doesn't."

"Is it then something too terrible—?"

She thought again. "I don't know what—for men—IS too terrible."

"Well then as you don't know what 'is' for women either—good-bye!" her visitor laughed.

It practically wound up the interview; which, however, terminating thus on a considerable stir of the air, was to give Miss Cutter for several days the sense of being much blown about. The degree to which, to begin with, she had been drawn—or perhaps rather pushed—closer to Scott was marked in the brief colloquy that she on her friend's departure had with him. He had immediately said it. "You'll see if she doesn't ask me down!"

"So soon?"

"Oh I've known them at places—at Cannes, at Pau, at Shanghai—do it sooner still. I always know when they will. You *can't* make out they don't love me!" He spoke almost plaintively, as if he wished she could.

"Then I don't see why it hasn't done you more good."

"Why Mamie," he patiently reasoned, "what more good *could* it? As I tell you," he explained, "it has just been my life."

"Then why do you come to me for money?"

"Oh they don't give me *that*!" Scott returned.

"So that it only means then, after all, that I, at the best, must keep you up?"

He fixed on her the nice eyes Lady Wantridge admired. "Do you mean to tell me that already—at this very moment—I'm not distinctly keeping you?"

She gave him back his look. "Wait till she *has* asked you, and then," Mamie added, "decline."

Scott, not too grossly, wondered. "As acting for *you*?"

Mamie's next injunction was answer enough. "But *before*—yes—call."

He took it in. "Call—but decline. Good!"

"The rest," she said, "I leave to you." And she left it in fact with such confidence that for a couple of days she was not only conscious of no need to give Mrs. Medwin another turn of the screw, but positively evaded, in her fortitude, the reappearance of that lady. It was not till the fourth day that she waited upon her, finding her, as she had expected, tense.

"Lady Wantridge *will*—?"

"Yes, though she says she won't."

"She says she won't? O-oh!" Mrs. Medwin moaned.

"Sit tight all the same. I *have* her!"

"But how?"

"Through Scott—whom she wants."

"Your bad brother!" Mrs. Medwin stared. "What does she want of him?"

"To amuse them at Catchmore. Anything for that. And he *would*. But he shan't!" Mamie declared. "He shan't go unless she comes. She must meet you first—you're my condition."

"O-o-oh!" Mrs. Medwin's tone was a wonder of hope and fear. "But doesn't he want to go?"

"He wants what I want. She draws the line at *you*. I draw the line at *him*."

"But *she*—doesn't she mind that he's bad?"

It was so artless that Mamie laughed. "No—it doesn't touch her. Besides, perhaps he isn't. It isn't as for you—people seem not to know. He has settled everything, at all events, by going to see her. It's before her that he's the thing she'll have to have."

"Have to?"

"For Sundays in the country. A feature—*the* feature."

"So she has asked him?"

"Yes—and he has declined."

"For ME?" Mrs. Medwin panted.

"For me," said Mamie on the door-step. "But I don't leave him for long." Her hansom had waited. "She'll come."

Lady Wantridge did come. She met in South Audley Street, on the fourteenth, at tea, the ladies whom Mamie had named to her, together with three or four others, and it was rather a master-stroke for Miss Cutter that if Mrs. Medwin was modestly present Scott Homer was as markedly not. This occasion, however, is a medal that would take rare casting, as would also, for that matter, even the minor light and shade, the lower relief, of the pecuniary transaction that Mrs. Medwin's flushed gratitude scarce awaited the dispersal of the company munificently to complete. A new understanding indeed on the spot rebounded from it, the conception of which, in Mamie's mind, had promptly bloomed. "He shan't go now unless he takes you." Then, as her fancy always moved quicker for her client than her client's own—"Down with him to Catchmore! When he goes to amuse them *you*," she serenely developed, "shall amuse them too." Mrs. Medwin's response was again rather oddly divided, but she was sufficiently intelligible when it came to meeting the hint that this latter provision would represent success to the tune of a separate fee. "Say," Mamie had suggested, "the same."

"Very well; the same."

The knowledge that it was to be the same had perhaps something to do also with the obliging spirit in which Scott eventually went. It was all at the last rather hurried—a party rapidly got together for the Grand Duke, who was in England but for the hour, who had good-naturedly proposed himself, and who liked his parties small, intimate and funny. This one was of the smallest and was finally judged to conform neither too little nor too much to the other conditions—after a brief whirlwind of wires and counterwires, and an iterated waiting of hansoms at various doors—to include Mrs. Medwin. It was from Catchmore itself that, snatching, a moment—on the wondrous Sunday afternoon, this lady had the harmonious thought of sending the new cheque. She was in bliss enough, but her scribble none the less intimated that it was Scott who amused them most. He *was* the feature.

THE ALTAR OF THE DEAD

CHAPTER I.

He had a mortal dislike, poor Stransom, to lean anniversaries, and loved them still less when they made a pretence of a figure. Celebrations and suppressions were equally painful to him, and but one of the former found a place in his life. He had kept each year in his own fashion the date of Mary Antrim's death. It would be more to the point perhaps to say that this occasion kept *him*: it kept him at least effectually from doing anything else. It took hold of him again and again with a hand of which time had softened but never loosened the touch. He waked to his feast of memory as consciously as he would have waked to his marriage-morn. Marriage had had of old but too little to say to the matter: for the girl who was to have been his bride there had been no bridal embrace. She had died of a malignant fever after the wedding-day had been fixed, and he had lost before fairly tasting it an affection that promised to fill his life to the brim.

Of that benediction, however, it would have been false to say this life could really be emptied: it was still ruled by a pale ghost, still ordered by a sovereign presence. He had not been a man of numerous passions, and even in all these years no sense had grown stronger with him than the sense of being bereft. He had needed no priest and no altar to make him for ever widowed. He had done many things in the world—he had done almost all but one: he had never, never forgotten. He had tried to put into his existence whatever else might take up room in it, but had failed to make it more than a house of which the mistress was eternally absent. She was most absent of all on the recurrent December day that his tenacity set apart. He had no arranged observance of it, but his nerves made it all their own. They drove him forth without mercy, and the goal of his pilgrimage was far. She had been buried in a London suburb, a part then of Nature's breast, but which he had seen lose one after another every feature of freshness. It was in truth during the moments he stood there that his eyes beheld the place least. They looked at another image, they opened to another light. Was it a credible future? Was it an incredible past? Whatever the answer it was an immense escape from the actual.

It's true that if there weren't other dates than this there were other memories; and by the time George Stransom was fifty-five such memories had greatly multiplied. There were other ghosts in his life than the ghost of Mary Antrim. He had perhaps not had more losses than most men, but he had counted his losses more; he hadn't seen death more closely, but had in a manner felt it more deeply. He had formed little by little the habit of numbering his Dead: it had come to him early in life that there was something one had to do for them. They were there in their simplified intensified essence, their conscious absence and expressive patience, as personally there as if they had only been stricken dumb. When all sense of them failed, all sound of them ceased, it was as if their purgatory were really still on earth: they asked so little that they got, poor things, even less, and died again, died every day, of the hard usage of life. They had no organised service, no reserved place, no honour, no shelter, no safety. Even ungenerous people provided for the living, but even those who were called most generous did nothing for the others. So on George Stransom's part had grown up with the years a resolve that he at least would do something, do it, that is, for his own—would perform the great charity without reproach. Every man *had* his own, and every man had, to meet this charity, the ample resources of the soul.

It was doubtless the voice of Mary Antrim that spoke for them best; as the years at any rate went by he found himself in regular communion with these postponed pensioners, those whom indeed he always called in his thoughts the Others. He spared them the moments, he organised the charity. Quite how it had risen he probably never could have told you, but what came to pass was that an altar, such as was after all within everybody's compass, lighted with perpetual candles and dedicated to these secret rites, reared itself in his spiritual spaces. He had wondered of old, in some embarrassment, whether he had a religion; being very sure, and not a little content, that he hadn't at all events the religion some of the people he had known wanted him to have. Gradually this question was straightened out for him: it became clear to him that the religion instilled by his earliest consciousness had been simply the religion of the Dead. It suited his inclination, it satisfied his spirit, it gave employment to his piety. It answered his love of great offices, of a solemn and splendid ritual; for no shrine could be more bedecked and no ceremonial more stately than those to which his worship was attached. He had no imagination about these things but that they were accessible to any one who should feel the need of them. The poorest could build such temples of the spirit—could make them blaze with candles and smoke with incense, make them flush with pictures and flowers. The cost, in the common phrase, of keeping them up fell wholly on the generous heart.

CHAPTER II.

He had this year, on the eve of his anniversary, as happened, an emotion not unconnected with that range of feeling. Walking home at the close of a busy day he was arrested in the London street by the particular effect of a shop-front that lighted the dull brown air with its mercenary grin and before which several persons were gathered. It was the window of a jeweller whose diamonds and sapphires seemed to laugh, in flashes like high notes of sound, with the mere joy of knowing how much more they were "worth" than most of the dingy pedestrians staring at them from the other side of the pane. Stransom lingered long enough to suspend, in a vision, a string of pearls about the white neck of Mary Antrim, and then was kept an instant longer by the sound of a voice he knew. Next him was a mumbling old woman, and beyond the old woman a gentleman with a lady on his arm. It was from him, from Paul Creston, the voice had proceeded: he was talking with the lady of some precious object in the window. Stransom had no sooner recognised him than the old woman turned away; but just with this growth of opportunity came a felt strangeness that stayed him in the very act of laying his hand on his friend's arm. It lasted but the instant, only that space sufficed for the flash of a wild question. Was *not* Mrs. Creston dead?—the ambiguity met him there in the short drop of her husband's voice, the drop conjugal, if it ever was, and in the way the two figures leaned to each other. Creston, making a step to look at something else, came nearer, glanced at him, started and exclaimed—behaviour the effect of which was at first only to leave Stransom staring, staring back across the months at the different face, the wholly other face, the poor man had shown him last, the blurred ravaged mask bent over the open grave by which they had stood together. That son of affliction wasn't in mourning now; he detached his arm from his companion's to grasp the hand of the older friend. He coloured as well as smiled in the strong light of the shop when Stransom raised a tentative hat to the lady. Stransom had just time to see she was pretty before he found himself gaping at a fact more portentous. "My dear fellow, let me make you acquainted with my wife."

Creston had blushed and stammered over it, but in half a minute, at the rate we live in polite society, it had practically become, for our friend, the mere memory of a shock. They stood there and laughed and talked; Stransom had instantly whisked the shock out of the way, to keep it for private consumption. He felt himself grimace, he heard himself exaggerate the proper, but was conscious of turning not a little faint. That new woman, that hired performer, Mrs. Creston? Mrs. Creston had been more living for him than any woman but one. This lady had a face that shone as publicly as the jeweller's window, and in the happy candour with which she wore her monstrous character was an effect of gross immodesty. The character of Paul Creston's wife thus attributed to her was monstrous for reasons Stransom could judge his friend to know perfectly that he knew. The happy pair had just arrived from America, and Stransom hadn't needed to be told this to guess the nationality of the lady. Somehow it deepened the foolish air that her husband's confused cordiality was unable to conceal. Stransom recalled that he had heard of poor Creston's having, while his bereavement was still fresh, crossed the sea for what people in such predicaments call a little change. He had found the little change indeed, he had brought the little change back; it was the little change that stood there and that, do what he would, he couldn't, while he showed those high front teeth of his, look other than a conscious ass about. They were going into the shop, Mrs. Creston said, and she begged Mr. Stransom to come with them and help to decide. He thanked her, opening his watch and pleading an engagement for which he was already late, and they parted while she shrieked into the fog, "Mind now you come to see me right away!" Creston had had the delicacy not to suggest that, and Stransom hoped it hurt him somewhere to hear her scream it to all the echoes.

He felt quite determined, as he walked away, never in his life to go near her. She was perhaps a human being, but Creston oughtn't to have shown her without precautions, oughtn't indeed to have shown her at all. His precautions should have been those of a forger or a murderer, and the people at home would never have mentioned extradition. This was a wife for foreign service or purely external use; a decent consideration would have spared her the injury of comparisons. Such was the first flush of George Stransom's reaction; but as he sat alone that night—there were particular

131

hours he always passed alone—the harshness dropped from it and left only the pity. *He* could spend an evening with Kate Creston, if the man to whom she had given everything couldn't. He had known her twenty years, and she was the only woman for whom he might perhaps have been unfaithful. She was all cleverness and sympathy and charm; her house had been the very easiest in all the world and her friendship the very firmest. Without accidents he had loved her, without accidents every one had loved her: she had made the passions about her as regular as the moon makes the tides. She had been also of course far too good for her husband, but he never suspected it, and in nothing had she been more admirable than in the exquisite art with which she tried to keep every one else (keeping Creston was no trouble) from finding it out. Here was a man to whom she had devoted her life and for whom she had given it up—dying to bring into the world a child of his bed; and she had had only to submit to her fate to have, ere the grass was green on her grave, no more existence for him than a domestic servant he had replaced. The frivolity, the indecency of it made Stransom's eyes fill; and he had that evening a sturdy sense that he alone, in a world without delicacy, had a right to hold up his head. While he smoked, after dinner, he had a book in his lap, but he had no eyes for his page: his eyes, in the swarming void of things, seemed to have caught Kate Creston's, and it was into their sad silences he looked. It was to him her sentient spirit had turned, knowing it to be of her he would think. He thought for a long time of how the closed eyes of dead women could still live—how they could open again, in a quiet lamplit room, long after they had looked their last. They had looks that survived—had them as great poets had quoted lines.

The newspaper lay by his chair—the thing that came in the afternoon and the servants thought one wanted; without sense for what was in it he had mechanically unfolded and then dropped it. Before he went to bed he took it up, and this time, at the top of a paragraph, he was caught by five words that made him start. He stood staring, before the fire, at the "Death of Sir Acton Hague, K.C.B.," the man who ten years earlier had been the nearest of his friends and whose deposition from this eminence had practically left it without an occupant. He had seen him after their rupture, but hadn't now seen him for years. Standing there before the fire he turned cold as he read what had befallen him. Promoted a short time previous to the governorship of the Westward Islands, Acton Hague had died, in the bleak honour of this exile, of an illness consequent on the bite of a poisonous snake. His career was compressed by the newspaper into a dozen lines, the perusal of which excited on George Stransom's part no warmer feeling than one of relief at the absence of any mention of their quarrel, an incident accidentally tainted at the time, thanks to their joint immersion in large affairs, with a horrible publicity. Public indeed was the wrong Stransom had, to his own sense, suffered, the insult he had blankly taken from the only man with whom he had ever been intimate; the friend, almost adored, of his University years, the subject, later, of his passionate loyalty: so public that he had never spoken of it to a human creature, so public that he had completely overlooked it. It had made the difference for him that friendship too was all over, but it had only made just that one. The shock of interests had been private, intensely so; but the action taken by Hague had been in the face of men. To-day it all seemed to have occurred merely to the end that George Stransom should think of him as "Hague" and measure exactly how much he himself could resemble a stone. He went cold, suddenly and horribly cold, to bed.

CHAPTER III.

The next day, in the afternoon, in the great grey suburb, he knew his long walk had tired him. In the dreadful cemetery alone he had been on his feet an hour. Instinctively, coming back, they had taken him a devious course, and it was a desert in which no circling cabman hovered over possible prey. He paused on a corner and measured the dreariness; then he made out through the gathered dusk that he was in one of those tracts of London which are less gloomy by night than by day, because, in the former case of the civil gift of light. By day there was nothing, but by night there were lamps, and George Stransom was in a mood that made lamps good in themselves. It wasn't that they could show him anything, it was only that they could burn clear. To his surprise, however, after a while, they did show him something: the arch of a high doorway approached by a low terrace of steps, in the depth of which—it formed a dim vestibule—the raising of a curtain at the moment he passed gave him a glimpse of an avenue of gloom with a glow of tapers at the end. He stopped and looked up, recognising the place as a church. The thought quickly came to him that since he was tired he might rest there; so that after a moment he had in turn pushed up the leathern curtain and gone in. It was a temple of the old persuasion, and there had evidently been a function—perhaps a service for the dead; the high altar was still a blaze of candles. This was an exhibition he always liked, and he dropped into a seat with relief. More than it had ever yet come home to him it struck him as good there should be churches.

This one was almost empty and the other altars were dim; a verger shuffled about, an old woman coughed, but it seemed to Stransom there was hospitality in the thick sweet air. Was it only the savour of the incense or was it something of larger intention? He had at any rate quitted the great grey suburb and come nearer to the warm centre. He presently ceased to feel intrusive, gaining at last even a sense of community with the only worshipper in his neighbourhood, the sombre presence of a woman, in mourning unrelieved, whose back was all he could see of her and who had sunk deep into prayer at no great distance from him. He wished he could sink, like her, to the very bottom, be as motionless, as rapt in prostration. After a few moments he shifted his seat; it was almost indelicate to be so aware of her. But Stransom subsequently quite lost himself, floating away on the sea of light. If occasions like this had been more frequent in his life he would have had more present the great original type, set up in a myriad temples, of the unapproachable shrine he had erected in his mind. That shrine had begun in vague likeness to church pomps, but the echo had ended by growing more distinct than the sound. The sound now rang out, the type blazed at him with all its fires and with a mystery of radiance in which endless meanings could glow. The thing became as he sat there his appropriate altar and each starry candle an appropriate vow. He numbered them, named them, grouped them—it was the silent roll-call of his Dead. They made together a brightness vast and intense, a brightness in which the mere chapel of his thoughts grew so dim that as it faded away he asked himself if he shouldn't find his real comfort in some material act, some outward worship.

This idea took possession of him while, at a distance, the black-robed lady continued prostrate; he was quietly thrilled with his conception, which at last brought him to his feet in the sudden excitement of a plan. He wandered softly through the aisles, pausing in the different chapels, all save one applied to a special devotion. It was in this clear recess, lampless and unapplied, that he stood longest—the length of time it took him fully to grasp the conception of gilding it with his bounty. He should snatch it from no other rites and associate it with nothing profane; he would simply take it as it should be given up to him and make it a masterpiece of splendour and a mountain of fire. Tended sacredly all the year, with the sanctifying church round it, it would always be ready for his offices. There would be difficulties, but from the first they presented themselves only as difficulties surmounted. Even for a person so little affiliated the thing would be a matter of arrangement. He saw it all in advance, and how bright in especial the place would become to him in the intermissions of toil and the dusk of afternoons; how rich in assurance at all times, but especially in the indifferent world. Before withdrawing he drew nearer again to the spot where he had first sat down, and in the movement he met the lady whom he had seen praying and who was now on her way to the door. She passed him quickly, and he had only a glimpse of her pale face and her unconscious, almost sightless eyes. For that instant she looked faded and handsome.

This was the origin of the rites more public, yet certainly esoteric, that he at last found himself able to establish. It took a long time, it took a year, and both the process and the result would have been—for any who knew—a vivid picture of his good faith. No one did know, in fact—no one but the bland ecclesiastics whose acquaintance he had promptly sought, whose objections he had softly overridden, whose curiosity and sympathy he had artfully charmed, whose assent to his eccentric munificence he had eventually won, and who had asked for concessions in exchange for indulgences. Stransom had of course at an early stage of his enquiry been referred to the Bishop, and the Bishop had been delightfully human, the Bishop had been almost amused. Success was within sight, at any rate from the moment the attitude of those whom it concerned became liberal in response to liberality. The altar and the sacred shell that half encircled it, consecrated to an ostensible and customary worship, were to be splendidly maintained; all that Stransom reserved to himself was the number of his lights and the free enjoyment of his intention. When the intention had taken complete effect the enjoyment became even greater than he had ventured to hope. He liked to think of this effect when far from it, liked to convince himself of it yet again when near. He was not often indeed so near as that a visit to it hadn't perforce something of the patience of a pilgrimage; but the time he gave to his devotion came to seem to him more a contribution to his other interests than a betrayal of them. Even a loaded life might be easier when one had added a new necessity to it.

How much easier was probably never guessed by those who simply knew there were hours when he disappeared and for many of whom there was a vulgar reading of what they used to call his plunges. These plunges were into depths quieter than the deep sea-caves, and the habit had at the end of a year or two become the one it would have cost him most to relinquish. Now they had really, his Dead, something that was indefensibly theirs; and he liked to think that they might in cases be the Dead of others, as well as that the Dead of others might be invoked there under the protection of what he had done. Whoever bent a knee on the carpet he had laid down appeared to him to act in the spirit of his intention. Each of his lights had a name for him, and from time to time a new light was kindled. This was what he had fundamentally agreed for, that there should always be room for them all. What those who passed or lingered saw was simply the most resplendent of the altars called suddenly into vivid usefulness, with a quiet elderly man, for whom it evidently had a fascination, often seated there in a maze or a doze; but half the satisfaction of the spot for this mysterious and fitful worshipper was that he found the years of his life there, and the ties, the affections, the struggles, the submissions, the conquests, if there had been such, a record of that adventurous journey in which the beginnings and the endings of human relations are the lettered mile-stones. He had in general little taste for the past as a part of his own history; at other times and in other places it mostly seemed to him pitiful to consider and impossible to repair; but on these occasions he accepted it with something of that positive gladness with which one adjusts one's self to an ache that begins to succumb to treatment. To the treatment of time the malady of life begins at a given moment to succumb; and these were doubtless the hours at which that truth most came home to him. The day was written for him there on which he had first become acquainted with death, and the successive phases of the acquaintance were marked each with a flame.

The flames were gathering thick at present, for Stransom had entered that dark defile of our earthly descent in which some one dies every day. It was only yesterday that Kate Creston had flashed out her white fire; yet already there were younger stars ablaze on the tips of the tapers. Various persons in whom his interest had not been intense drew closer to him by entering this company. He went over it, head by head, till he felt like the shepherd of a huddled flock, with all a shepherd's vision of differences imperceptible. He knew his candles apart, up to the colour of the flame, and would still have known them had their positions all been changed. To other imaginations they might stand for other things—that they should stand for something to be hushed before was all he desired; but he was intensely conscious of the personal note of each and of the distinguishable way it contributed to the concert. There were hours at which he almost caught himself wishing that certain of his friends would now die, that he might establish with them in this manner a connexion more charming than, as it happened, it was possible to enjoy with them in life. In regard to those from whom one was separated by the long curves of the globe such a connexion could only be an improvement: it brought them instantly within reach. Of course there were gaps in the constellation, for Stransom knew he could only pretend to act for his own, and it wasn't every figure passing before his eyes into the great obscure that was entitled to a memorial. There was a strange sanctification in death, but some characters were more sanctified by being forgotten than by being remembered. The greatest blank in the shining page was the memory of Acton Hague, of which he inveterately tried to rid himself. For Acton Hague no flame could ever rise on any altar of his.

CHAPTER IV.

Every year, the day he walked back from the great graveyard, he went to church as he had done the day his idea was born. It was on this occasion, as it happened, after a year had passed, that he began to observe his altar to be haunted by a worshipper at least as frequent as himself. Others of the faithful, and in the rest of the church, came and went, appealing sometimes, when they disappeared, to a vague or to a particular recognition; but this unfailing presence was always to be observed when he arrived and still in possession when he departed. He was surprised, the first time, at the promptitude with which it assumed an identity for him—the identity of the lady whom two years before, on his anniversary, he had seen so intensely bowed, and of whose tragic face he had had so flitting a vision. Given the time that had passed, his recollection of her was fresh enough to make him wonder. Of himself she had of course no impression, or rather had had none at first: the time came when her manner of transacting her business suggested her having gradually guessed his call to be of the same order. She used his altar for her own purpose—he could only hope that sad and solitary as she always struck him, she used it for her own Dead. There were interruptions, infidelities, all on his part, calls to other associations and duties; but as the months went on he found her whenever he returned, and he ended by taking pleasure in the thought that he had given her almost the contentment he had given himself. They worshipped side by side so often that there were moments when he wished he might be sure, so straight did their prospect stretch away of growing old together in their rites. She was younger than he, but she looked as if her Dead were at least as numerous as his candles. She had no colour, no sound, no fault, and another of the things about which he had made up his mind was that she had no fortune. Always black-robed, she must have had a succession of sorrows. People weren't poor, after all, whom so many losses could overtake; they were positively rich when they had had so much to give up. But the air of this devoted and indifferent woman, who always made, in any attitude, a beautiful accidental line, conveyed somehow to Stransom that she had known more kinds of trouble than one.

He had a great love of music and little time for the joy of it; but occasionally, when workaday noises were muffled by Saturday afternoons it used to come back to him that there were glories. There were moreover friends who reminded him of this and side by side with whom he found himself sitting out concerts. On one of these winter afternoons, in St. James's Hall, he became aware after he had seated himself that the lady he had so often seen at church was in the place next him and was evidently alone, as he also this time happened to be. She was at first too absorbed in the consideration of the programme to heed him, but when she at last glanced at him he took advantage of the movement to speak to her, greeting her with the remark that he felt as if he already knew her. She smiled as she said "Oh yes, I recognise you"; yet in spite of this admission of long acquaintance it was the first he had seen of her smile. The effect of it was suddenly to contribute more to that acquaintance than all the previous meetings had done. He hadn't "taken in," he said to himself, that she was so pretty. Later, that evening—it was while he rolled along in a hansom on his way to dine out—he added that he hadn't taken in that she was so interesting. The next morning in the midst of his work he quite suddenly and irrelevantly reflected that his impression of her, beginning so far back, was like a winding river that had at last reached the sea.

His work in fact was blurred a little all that day by the sense of what had now passed between them. It wasn't much, but it had just made the difference. They had listened together to Beethoven and Schumann; they had talked in the pauses, and at the end, when at the door, to which they moved together, he had asked her if he could help her in the matter of getting away. She had thanked him and put up her umbrella, slipping into the crowd without an allusion to their meeting yet again and leaving him to remember at leisure that not a word had been exchanged about the usual scene of that coincidence. This omission struck him now as natural and then again as perverse. She mightn't in the least have allowed his warrant for speaking to her, and yet if she hadn't he would have judged her an underbred woman. It was odd that when nothing had really ever brought them together he should have been able successfully to assume they were in a manner old friends—that this negative quantity was somehow more than they could express. His success, it was true, had been qualified by her quick escape, so that there grew up in him an absurd desire to put it to some better test. Save in so far as some other poor chance might help him, such a test could be only to meet her afresh at church. Left to himself he would have gone to church the very next afternoon, just for the curiosity of seeing if he should find her there. But he wasn't left to himself, a fact he discovered quite at the last, after he had virtually made up his mind to go. The influence that kept him away really revealed to him how little to himself his Dead *ever* left him. He went only for *them*—for nothing else in the world.

The force of this revulsion kept him away ten days: he hated to connect the place with anything but his offices or to give a glimpse of the curiosity that had been on the point of moving him. It was absurd to weave a tangle about a matter so simple as a custom of devotion that might with ease have been daily or hourly; yet the tangle got itself woven. He was sorry, he was disappointed: it was as if a long happy spell had been broken and he had lost a familiar security. At the last, however, he asked himself if he was to stay away for ever from the fear of this muddle about motives. After an interval neither longer nor shorter than usual he re-entered the church with a clear conviction that he should scarcely heed the presence or the absence of the lady of the concert. This indifference didn't prevent his at once noting that for the only time since he had first seen her she wasn't on the spot. He had now no scruple about giving her time to arrive, but she didn't arrive, and when he went away still missing her he was profanely and consentingly sorry. If her absence made the tangle more intricate, that was all her own doing. By the end of another year it was very intricate indeed; but by that time he didn't in the least care, and it was only his cultivated consciousness that had given him scruples. Three times in three months he had gone to church without finding her, and he felt he hadn't needed these occasions to show him his suspense had dropped. Yet it was, incongruously, not indifference, but a refinement of delicacy that had kept him from asking the sacristan, who would of course immediately have recognised his description of her, whether she had been seen at other hours. His delicacy had kept him from asking any question about her at any time, and it was exactly the same virtue that had left him so free to be decently civil to her at the concert.

This happy advantage now served him anew, enabling him when she finally met his eyes—it was after a fourth trial—to predetermine quite fixedly his awaiting her retreat. He joined her in the street as soon as she had moved, asking her if he might accompany her a certain distance. With her placid permission he went as far as a house in the neighbourhood at which she had business: she let him know it was not where she lived. She lived, as she said, in a mere slum, with an old aunt, a person in connexion with whom she spoke of the engrossment of humdrum duties and regular occupations. She wasn't, the mourning niece, in her first youth, and her vanished freshness had left something behind that, for Stransom, represented the proof it had been tragically sacrificed. Whatever she gave him the assurance of she gave without references. She might have been a divorced duchess—she might have been an old maid who taught the harp.

CHAPTER V.

They fell at last into the way of walking together almost every time they met, though for a long time still they never met but at church. He couldn't ask her to come and see him, and as if she hadn't a proper place to receive him she never invited her friend. As much as himself she knew the world of London, but from an undiscussed instinct of privacy they haunted the region not mapped on the social chart. On the return she always made him leave her at the same corner. She looked with him, as a pretext for a pause, at the depressed things in suburban shop-fronts; and there was never a word he had said to her that she hadn't beautifully understood. For long ages he never knew her name, any more than she had ever pronounced his own; but it was not their names that mattered, it was only their perfect practice and their common need.

These things made their whole relation so impersonal that they hadn't the rules or reasons people found in ordinary friendships. They didn't care for the things it was supposed necessary to care for in the intercourse of the world. They ended one day—they never knew which of them expressed it first—by throwing out the idea that they didn't care for each other. Over this idea they grew quite intimate; they rallied to it in a way that marked a fresh start in their confidence. If to feel deeply together about certain things wholly distinct from themselves didn't constitute a safety, where was safety to be looked for? Not lightly nor often, not without occasion nor without emotion, any more than in any other reference by serious people to a mystery of their faith; but when something had happened to warm, as it were, the air for it, they came as near as they could come to calling their Dead by name. They felt it was coming very near to utter their thought at all. The word "they" expressed enough; it limited the mention, it had a dignity of its own, and if, in their talk, you had heard our friends use it, you might have taken them for a pair of pagans of old alluding decently to the domesticated gods. They never knew—at least Stransom never knew—how they had learned to be sure about each other. If it had been with each a question of what the other was there for, the certitude had come in some fine way of its own. Any faith, after all, has the instinct of propagation, and it was as natural as it was beautiful that they should have taken pleasure on the spot in the imagination of a following. If the following was for each but a following of one it had proved in the event sufficient. Her debt, however, of course was much greater than his, because while she had only given him a worshipper he had given her a splendid temple. Once she said she pitied him for the length of his list— she had counted his candles almost as often as himself—and this made him wonder what could have been the length of hers. He had wondered before at the coincidence of their losses, especially as from time to time a new candle was set up. On some occasion some accident led him to express this curiosity, and she answered as if in surprise that he hadn't already understood. "Oh for me, you know, the more there are the better—there could never be too many. I should like hundreds and hundreds—I should like thousands; I should like a great mountain of light."

Then of course in a flash he understood. "Your Dead are only One?"

She hung back at this as never yet. "Only One," she answered, colouring as if now he knew her guarded secret. It really made him feel he knew less than before, so difficult was it for him to reconstitute a life in which a single experience had so belittled all others. His own life, round its central hollow, had been packed close enough. After this she appeared to have regretted her confession, though at the moment she spoke there had been pride in her very embarrassment. She declared to him that his own was the larger, the dearer possession—the portion one would have chosen if one had been able to choose; she assured him she could perfectly imagine some of the echoes with which his silences were peopled. He knew she couldn't: one's relation to what one had loved and hated had been a relation too distinct from the relations of others. But this didn't affect the fact that they were growing old together in their piety. She was a feature of that piety, but even at the ripe stage of acquaintance in which they occasionally arranged to meet at a concert or to go together to an exhibition she was not a feature of anything else. The most that happened was that his worship became paramount. Friend by friend dropped away till at last there were more emblems on his altar than houses left him to enter. She was more than any other the friend who remained, but she was unknown to all the rest. Once when she had discovered, as they called it, a new star, she used the expression that the chapel at last was full.

"Oh no," Stransom replied, "there is a great thing wanting for that! The chapel will never be full till a candle is set up before which all the others will pale. It will be the tallest candle of all."

Her mild wonder rested on him. "What candle do you mean?"

"I mean, dear lady, my own."

He had learned after a long time that she earned money by her pen, writing under a pseudonym she never disclosed in magazines he never saw. She knew too well what he couldn't read and what she couldn't write, and she taught him to cultivate indifference with a success that did much for their good relations. Her invisible industry was a convenience to him; it helped his contented thought of her, the thought that rested in the dignity of her proud obscure life, her little remunerated art and her little impenetrable home. Lost, with her decayed relative, in her dim suburban world, she came to the surface for him in distant places. She was really the priestess of his altar, and whenever he quitted England he committed it to her keeping. She proved to him afresh that women have more of the spirit of religion than men; he felt his fidelity pale and faint in comparison with hers. He often said to her that since he had so little time to live he rejoiced in her having so much; so glad was he to think she would guard the temple when he should have been called. He had a great plan for that, which of course he told her too, a bequest of money to keep it up in undiminished state. Of the administration of this fund he would appoint her superintendent, and if the spirit should move her she might kindle a taper even for him.

"And who will kindle one even for me?" she then seriously asked.

CHAPTER VI.

She was always in mourning, yet the day he came back from the longest absence he had yet made her appearance immediately told him she had lately had a bereavement. They met on this occasion as she was leaving the church, so that postponing his own entrance he instantly offered to turn round and walk away with her. She considered, then she said: "Go in now, but come and see me in an hour." He knew the small vista of her street, closed at the end and as dreary as an empty pocket, where the pairs of shabby little houses, semi-detached but indissolubly united, were like married couples on bad terms. Often, however, as he had gone to the beginning he had never gone beyond. Her aunt was dead—that he immediately guessed, as well as that it made a difference; but when she had for the first time mentioned her number he found himself, on her leaving him, not a little agitated by this sudden liberality. She wasn't a person with whom, after all, one got on so very fast: it had taken him months and months to learn her name, years and years to learn her address. If she had looked, on this reunion, so much older to him, how in the world did he look to her? She had reached the period of life he had long since reached, when, after separations, the marked clock-face of the friend we meet announces the hour we have tried to forget. He couldn't have said what he expected as, at the end of his waiting, he turned the corner where for years he had always paused; simply not to pause was a efficient cause for emotion. It was an event, somehow; and in all their long acquaintance there had never been an event. This one grew larger when, five minutes later, in the faint elegance of her little drawing-room, she quavered out a greeting that showed the measure she took of it. He had a strange sense of having come for something in particular; strange because literally there was nothing particular between them, nothing save that they were at one on their great point, which had long ago become a magnificent matter of course. It was true that after she had said "You can always come now, you know," the thing he was there for seemed already to have happened. He asked her if it was the death of her aunt that made the difference; to which she replied: "She never knew I knew you. I wished her not to." The beautiful clearness of her candour—her faded beauty was like a summer twilight—disconnected the words from any image of deceit. They might have struck him as the record of a deep dissimulation; but she had always given him a sense of noble reasons. The vanished aunt was present, as he looked about him, in the small complacencies of the room, the beaded velvet and the fluted moreen; and though, as we know, he had the worship of the Dead, he found himself not definitely regretting this lady. If she wasn't in his long list, however, she was in her niece's short one, and Stransom presently observed to the latter that now at least, in the place they haunted together, she would have another object of devotion.

"Yes, I shall have another. She was very kind to me. It's that that's the difference."

He judged, wondering a good deal before he made any motion to leave her, that the difference would somehow be very great and would consist of still other things than her having let him come in. It rather chilled him, for they had been happy together as they were. He extracted from her at any rate an intimation that she should now have means less limited, that her aunt's tiny fortune had come to her, so that there was henceforth only one to consume what had formerly been made to suffice for two. This was a joy to Stransom, because it had hitherto been equally impossible for him either to offer her presents or contentedly to stay his hand. It was too ugly to be at her side that way, abounding himself and yet not able to overflow—a demonstration that would have been signally a false note. Even her better situation too seemed only to draw out in a sense the loneliness of her future. It would merely help her to live more and more for their small ceremonial, and this at a time when he himself had begun wearily to feel that, having set it in motion, he might depart. When they had sat a while in the pale parlour she got up—"This isn't my room: let us go into mine." They had only to cross the narrow hall, as he found, to pass quite into another air. When she had closed the door of the second room, as she called it, he felt at last in real possession of her. The place had the flush of life—it was expressive; its dark red walls were articulate with memories and relics. These were simple things—photographs and water-colours, scraps of writing framed and ghosts of flowers embalmed;

but a moment sufficed to show him they had a common meaning. It was here she had lived and worked, and she had already told him she would make no change of scene. He read the reference in the objects about her—the general one to places and times; but after a minute he distinguished among them a small portrait of a gentleman. At a distance and without their glasses his eyes were only so caught by it as to feel a vague curiosity. Presently this impulse carried him nearer, and in another moment he was staring at the picture in stupefaction and with the sense that some sound had broken from him. He was further conscious that he showed his companion a white face when he turned round on her gasping: "Acton Hague!"

She matched his great wonder. "Did you know him?"

"He was the friend of all my youth—of my early manhood. And *you* knew him?"

She coloured at this and for a moment her answer failed; her eyes embraced everything in the place, and a strange irony reached her lips as she echoed: "Knew him?"

Then Stransom understood, while the room heaved like the cabin of a ship, that its whole contents cried out with him, that it was a museum in his honour, that all her later years had been addressed to him and that the shrine he himself had reared had been passionately converted to this use. It was all for Acton Hague that she had kneeled every day at his altar. What need had there been for a consecrated candle when he was present in the whole array? The revelation so smote our friend in the face that he dropped into a seat and sat silent. He had quickly felt her shaken by the force of his shock, but as she sank on the sofa beside him and laid her hand on his arm he knew almost as soon that she mightn't resent it as much as she'd have liked.

CHAPTER VII.

He learned in that instant two things: one being that even in so long a time she had gathered no knowledge of his great intimacy and his great quarrel; the other that in spite of this ignorance, strangely enough, she supplied on the spot a reason for his stupor. "How extraordinary," he presently exclaimed, "that we should never have known!"

She gave a wan smile which seemed to Stransom stranger even than the fact itself. "I never, never spoke of him."

He looked again about the room. "Why then, if your life had been so full of him?"

"Mayn't I put you that question as well? Hadn't your life also been full of him?"

"Any one's, every one's life who had the wonderful experience of knowing him. *I* never spoke of him," Stransom added in a moment, "because he did me—years ago—an unforgettable wrong." She was silent, and with the full effect of his presence all about them it almost startled her guest to hear no protest escape her. She accepted his words, he turned his eyes to her again to see in what manner she accepted them. It was with rising tears and a rare sweetness in the movement of putting out her hand to take his own. Nothing more wonderful had ever appeared to him than, in that little chamber of remembrance and homage, to see her convey with such exquisite mildness that as from Acton Hague any injury was credible. The clock ticked in the stillness—Hague had probably given it to her—and while he let her hold his hand with a tenderness that was almost an assumption of responsibility for his old pain as well as his new, Stransom after a minute broke out: "Good God, how he must have used *you!*"

She dropped his hand at this, got up and, moving across the room, made straight a small picture to which, on examining it, he had given a slight push. Then turning round on him with her pale gaiety recovered, "I've forgiven him!" she declared.

"I know what you've done," said Stransom "I know what you've done for years." For a moment they looked at each other through it all with their long community of service in their eyes. This short passage made, to his sense, for the woman before him, an immense, an absolutely naked confession; which was presently, suddenly blushing red and changing her place again, what she appeared to learn he perceived in it. He got up and "How you must have loved him!" he cried.

"Women aren't like men. They can love even where they've suffered."

"Women are wonderful," said Stransom. "But I assure you I've forgiven him too."

"If I had known of anything so strange I wouldn't have brought you here."

"So that we might have gone on in our ignorance to the last?"

"What do you call the last?" she asked, smiling still.

At this he could smile back at her. "You'll see—when it comes."

She thought of that. "This is better perhaps; but as we were—it was good."

He put her the question. "Did it never happen that he spoke of me?"

Considering more intently she made no answer, and he then knew he should have been adequately answered by her asking how often he himself had spoken of their terrible friend. Suddenly a brighter light broke in her face and an excited idea sprang to her lips in the appeal: "You *have* forgiven him?"

"How, if I hadn't, could I linger here?"

She visibly winced at the deep but unintended irony of this; but even while she did so she panted quickly: "Then in the lights on your altar—?"

"There's never a light for Acton Hague!"

She stared with a dreadful fall, "But if he's one of your Dead?"

"He's one of the world's, if you like—he's one of yours. But he's not one of mine. Mine are only the Dead who died possessed of me. They're mine in death because they were mine in life."

"*He* was yours in life then, even if for a while he ceased to be. If you forgave him you went back to him. Those whom we've once loved—"

"Are those who can hurt us most," Stransom broke in.

"Ah it's not true—you've *not* forgiven him!" she wailed with a passion that startled him.

He looked at her as never yet. "What was it he did to you?"

"Everything!" Then abruptly she put out her hand in farewell. "Good-bye."

He turned as cold as he had turned that night he read the man's death. "You mean that we meet no more?"

"Not as we've met—not *there*!"

He stood aghast at this snap of their great bond, at the renouncement that rang out in the word she so expressively sounded. "But what's changed—for you?"

She waited in all the sharpness of a trouble that for the first time since he had known her made her splendidly stern. "How can you understand now when you didn't understand before?"

"I didn't understand before only because I didn't know. Now that I know, I see what I've been living with for years," Stransom went on very gently.

She looked at him with a larger allowance, doing this gentleness justice. "How can I then, on this new knowledge of my own, ask you to continue to live with it?"

"I set up my altar, with its multiplied meanings," Stransom began; but she quietly interrupted him.

"You set up your altar, and when I wanted one most I found it magnificently ready. I used it with the gratitude I've always shown you, for I knew it from of old to be dedicated to Death. I told you long ago that my Dead weren't many. Yours were, but all you had done for them was none too much for *my* worship! You had placed a great light for Each—I gathered them together for One!"

"We had simply different intentions," he returned. "That, as you say, I perfectly knew, and I don't see why your intention shouldn't still sustain you."

"That's because you're generous—you can imagine and think. But the spell is broken."

It seemed to poor Stransom, in spite of his resistance, that it really was, and the prospect stretched grey and void before him. All he could say, however, was: "I hope you'll try before you give up."

"If I had known you had ever known him I should have taken for granted he had his candle," she presently answered. "What's changed, as you say, is that on making the discovery I find he never has had it. That makes *my* attitude"—she paused as thinking how to express it, then said simply—"all wrong."

"Come once again," he pleaded.

"Will you give him his candle?" she asked.

He waited, but only because it would sound ungracious; not because of a doubt of his feeling. "I can't do that!" he declared at last.

"Then good-bye." And she gave him her hand again.

He had got his dismissal; besides which, in the agitation of everything that had opened out to him, he felt the need to recover himself as he could only do in solitude. Yet he lingered—lingered to see if she had no compromise to express, no attenuation to propose. But he only met her great lamenting eyes, in which indeed he read that she was as sorry for him as for any one else. This made him say: "At least, in any case, I may see you here."

"Oh yes, come if you like. But I don't think it will do."

He looked round the room once more, knowing how little he was sure it would do. He felt also stricken and more and more cold, and his chill was like an ague in which he had to make an effort not to shake. Then he made doleful reply: "I must try on my side—if you can't try on yours." She came out with him to the hall and into the doorway, and here he put her the question he held he could least answer from his own wit. "Why have you never let me come before?"

"Because my aunt would have seen you, and I should have had to tell her how I came to know you."

"And what would have been the objection to that?"

"It would have entailed other explanations; there would at any rate have been that danger."

"Surely she knew you went every day to church," Stransom objected.

"She didn't know what I went for."

"Of me then she never even heard?"

"You'll think I was deceitful. But I didn't need to be!"

He was now on the lower door-step, and his hostess held the door half-closed behind him. Through what remained of the opening he saw her framed face. He made a supreme appeal. "What *did* he do to you?"

"It would have come out—*she* would have told you. That fear at my heart—that was my reason!" And she closed the door, shutting him out.

CHAPTER VIII.

He had ruthlessly abandoned her—that of course was what he had done. Stransom made it all out in solitude, at leisure, fitting the unmatched pieces gradually together and dealing one by one with a hundred obscure points. She had known Hague only after her present friend's relations with him had wholly terminated; obviously indeed a good while after; and it was natural enough that of his previous life she should have ascertained only what he had judged good to communicate. There were passages it was quite conceivable that even in moments of the tenderest expansion he should have withheld. Of many facts in the career of a man so in the eye of the world there was of course a common knowledge; but this lady lived apart from public affairs, and the only time perfectly clear to her would have been the time following the dawn of her own drama. A man in her place would have "looked up" the past—would even have consulted old newspapers. It remained remarkable indeed that in her long contact with the partner of her retrospect no accident had lighted a train; but there was no arguing about that; the accident had in fact come: it had simply been that security had prevailed. She had taken what Hague had given her, and her blankness in respect of his other connexions was only a touch in the picture of that plasticity Stransom had supreme reason to know so great a master could have been trusted to produce.

This picture was for a while all our friend saw: he caught his breath again and again as it came over him that the woman with whom he had had for years so fine a point of contact was a woman whom Acton Hague, of all men in the world, had more or less fashioned. Such as she sat there to-day she was ineffaceably stamped with him. Beneficent, blameless as Stransom held her, he couldn't rid himself of the sense that he had been, as who should say, swindled. She had imposed upon him hugely, though she had known it as little as he. All this later past came back to him as a time grotesquely misspent. Such at least were his first reflexions; after a while he found himself more divided and only, as the end of it, more troubled. He imagined, recalled, reconstituted, figured out for himself the truth she had refused to give him;

the effect of which was to make her seem to him only more saturated with her fate. He felt her spirit, through the whole strangeness, finer than his own to the very degree in which she might have been, in which she certainly had been, more wronged. A women, when wronged, was always more wronged than a man, and there were conditions when the least she could have got off with was more than the most he could have to bear. He was sure this rare creature wouldn't have got off with the least. He was awestruck at the thought of such a surrender—such a prostration. Moulded indeed she had been by powerful hands, to have converted her injury into an exaltation so sublime. The fellow had only had to die for everything that was ugly in him to be washed out in a torrent. It was vain to try to guess what had taken place, but nothing could be clearer than that she had ended by accusing herself. She absolved him at every point, she adored her very wounds. The passion by which he had profited had rushed back after its ebb, and now the tide of tenderness, arrested for ever at flood, was too deep even to fathom. Stransom sincerely considered that he had forgiven him; but how little he had achieved the miracle that she had achieved! His forgiveness was silence, but hers was mere unuttered sound. The light she had demanded for his altar would have broken his silence with a blare; whereas all the lights in the church were for her too great a hush.

She had been right about the difference—she had spoken the truth about the change: Stransom was soon to know himself as perversely but sharply jealous. *His* tide had ebbed, not flowed; if he had "forgiven" Acton Hague, that forgiveness was a motive with a broken spring. The very fact of her appeal for a material sign, a sign that should make her dead lover equal there with the others, presented the concession to her friend as too handsome for the case. He had never thought of himself as hard, but an exorbitant article might easily render him so. He moved round and round this one, but only in widening circles—the more he looked at it the less acceptable it seemed. At the same time he had no illusion about the effect of his refusal; he perfectly saw how it would make for a rupture. He left her alone a week, but when at last he again called this conviction was cruelly confirmed. In the interval he had kept away from the church, and he needed no fresh assurance from her to know she hadn't entered it. The change was complete enough:

it had broken up her life. Indeed it had broken up his, for all the fires of his shrine seemed to him suddenly to have been quenched. A great indifference fell upon him, the weight of which was in itself a pain; and he never knew what his devotion had been for him till in that shock it ceased like a dropped watch. Neither did he know with how large a confidence he had counted on the final service that had now failed: the mortal deception was that in this abandonment the whole future gave way.

These days of her absence proved to him of what she was capable; all the more that he never dreamed she was vindictive or even resentful. It was not in anger she had forsaken him; it was in simple submission to hard reality, to the stern logic of life. This came home to him when he sat with her again in the room in which her late aunt's conversation lingered like the tone of a cracked piano. She tried to make him forget how much they were estranged, but in the very presence of what they had given up it was impossible not to be sorry for her. He had taken from her so much more than she had taken from him. He argued with her again, told her she could now have the altar to herself; but she only shook her head with pleading sadness, begging him not to waste his breath on the impossible, the extinct. Couldn't he see that in relation to her private need the rites he had established were practically an elaborate exclusion? She regretted nothing that had happened; it had all been right so long as she didn't know, and it was only that now she knew too much and that from the moment their eyes were open they would simply have to conform. It had doubtless been happiness enough for them to go on together so long. She was gentle, grateful, resigned; but this was only the form of a deep immoveability. He saw he should never more cross the threshold of the second room, and he felt how much this alone would make a stranger of him and give a conscious stiffness to his visits. He would have hated to plunge again into that well of reminders, but he enjoyed quite as little the vacant alternative.

After he had been with her three or four times it struck him that to have come at last into her house had had the horrid effect of diminishing their intimacy. He had known her better, had liked her in greater freedom, when they merely walked together or kneeled together. Now they only pretended;

before they had been nobly sincere. They began to try their walks again, but it proved a lame imitation, for these things, from the first, beginning or ending, had been connected with their visits to the church. They had either strolled away as they came out or gone in to rest on the return. Stransom, besides, now faltered; he couldn't walk as of old. The omission made everything false; it was a dire mutilation of their lives. Our friend was frank and monotonous, making no mystery of his remonstrance and no secret of his predicament. Her response, whatever it was, always came to the same thing—an implied invitation to him to judge, if he spoke of predicaments, of how much comfort she had in hers. For him indeed was no comfort even in complaint, since every allusion to what had befallen them but made the author of their trouble more present. Acton Hague was between them—that was the essence of the matter, and never so much between them as when they were face to face. Then Stransom, while still wanting to banish him, had the strangest sense of striving for an ease that would involve having accepted him. Deeply disconcerted by what he knew, he was still worse tormented by really not knowing. Perfectly aware that it would have been horribly vulgar to abuse his old friend or to tell his companion the story of their quarrel, it yet vexed him that her depth of reserve should give him no opening and should have the effect of a magnanimity greater even than his own.

He challenged himself, denounced himself, asked himself if he were in love with her that he should care so much what adventures she had had. He had never for a moment allowed he was in love with her; therefore nothing could have surprised him more than to discover he was jealous. What but jealousy could give a man that sore contentious wish for the detail of what would make him suffer? Well enough he knew indeed that he should never have it from the only person who to-day could give it to him. She let him press her with his sombre eyes, only smiling at him with an exquisite mercy and breathing equally little the word that would expose her secret and the word that would appear to deny his literal right to bitterness. She told nothing, she judged nothing; she accepted everything but the possibility of her return to the old symbols. Stransom divined that for her too they had been vividly individual, had stood for particular hours or particular attributes— particular links in her chain. He made it clear to himself, as he believed, that his difficulty lay in the fact that the very nature of the plea for his faithless friend constituted a prohibition; that it happened to have come from *her* was precisely the vice that attached to it. To the voice of impersonal generosity he felt sure he would have listened; he would have deferred to an advocate who, speaking from abstract justice, knowing of his denial without having known Hague, should have had the imagination to say: "Ah, remember only the best of him; pity him; provide for him." To provide for him on the very ground of having discovered another of his turpitudes was not to pity but to glorify him. The more Stransom thought the more he made out that whatever this relation of Hague's it could only have been a deception more or less finely practised. Where had it come into the life that all men saw? Why had one never heard of it if it had had the frankness of honourable things? Stransom knew enough of his other ties, of his obligations and appearances, not to say enough of his general character, to be sure there had been some infamy. In one way or another this creature had been coldly sacrificed. That was why at the last as well as the first he must still leave him out and out.

CHAPTER IX.

And yet this was no solution, especially after he had talked again to his friend of all it had been his plan she should finally do for him. He had talked in the other days, and she had responded with a frankness qualified only by a courteous reluctance, a reluctance that touched him, to linger on the question of his death. She had then practically accepted the charge, suffered him to feel he could depend upon her to be the eventual guardian of his shrine; and it was in the name of what had so passed between them that he appealed to her not to forsake him in his age. She listened at present with shining coldness and all her habitual forbearance to insist on her terms; her deprecation was even still tenderer, for it expressed the compassion of her own sense that he was abandoned. Her terms, however, remained the same, and scarcely the less audible for not being uttered; though he was sure that secretly even more than he she felt bereft of the satisfaction his solemn trust was to have provided her. They both missed the rich future, but she missed it most, because after all it was to have been entirely hers; and it was her acceptance of the loss that gave him the full measure of her preference for the thought of Acton Hague over any other thought whatever. He had humour enough to laugh rather grimly when he said to himself: "Why the deuce does she like him so much more than she likes me?"—the reasons being really so conceivable. But even his faculty of analysis left the irritation standing, and this irritation proved perhaps the greatest misfortune that had ever overtaken him. There had been nothing yet that made him so much want to give up. He had of course by this time well reached the age of renouncement; but it had not hitherto been vivid to him that it was time to give up everything.

Practically, at the end of six months, he had renounced the friendship once so charming and comforting. His privation had two faces, and the face it had turned to him on the occasion of his last attempt to cultivate that friendship was the one he could look at least. This was the privation he inflicted; the other was the privation he bore. The conditions she never phrased he used to murmur to himself in solitude: "One more, one more—

only just one." Certainly he was going down; he often felt it when he caught himself, over his work, staring at vacancy and giving voice to that inanity. There was proof enough besides in his being so weak and so ill. His irritation took the form of melancholy, and his melancholy that of the conviction that his health had quite failed. His altar moreover had ceased to exist; his chapel, in his dreams, was a great dark cavern. All the lights had gone out—all his Dead had died again. He couldn't exactly see at first how it had been in the power of his late companion to extinguish them, since it was neither for her nor by her that they had been called into being. Then he understood that it was essentially in his own soul the revival had taken place, and that in the air of this soul they were now unable to breathe. The candles might mechanically burn, but each of them had lost its lustre. The church had become a void; it was his presence, her presence, their common presence, that had made the indispensable medium. If anything was wrong everything was—her silence spoiled the tune.

Then when three months were gone he felt so lonely that he went back; reflecting that as they had been his best society for years his Dead perhaps wouldn't let him forsake them without doing something more for him. They stood there, as he had left them, in their tall radiance, the bright cluster that had already made him, on occasions when he was willing to compare small things with great, liken them to a group of sea-lights on the edge of the ocean of life. It was a relief to him, after a while, as he sat there, to feel they had still a virtue. He was more and more easily tired, and he always drove now; the action of his heart was weak and gave him none of the reassurance conferred by the action of his fancy. None the less he returned yet again, returned several times, and finally, during six months, haunted the place with a renewal of frequency and a strain of impatience. In winter the church was unwarmed and exposure to cold forbidden him, but the glow of his shrine was an influence in which he could almost bask. He sat and wondered to what he had reduced his absent associate and what she now did with the hours of her absence. There were other churches, there were other altars, there were other candles; in one way or another her piety would still operate; he couldn't absolutely have deprived her of her rites. So he argued, but without contentment; for he well enough knew there was no other such rare semblance of the mountain of light she had once mentioned to him as the satisfaction of her need. As this semblance again gradually grew great to him and his pious practice more regular, he found a sharper and sharper pang in the imagination of her darkness; for never so much as in these weeks had his rites been real, never had his gathered company seemed so to respond and even to invite. He lost himself in the large lustre, which was more and more what he had from the first wished it to be—as dazzling as the vision of heaven in the mind of a child. He wandered in the fields of light; he passed, among the tall tapers, from tier to tier, from fire to fire, from name to name, from the white intensity of one clear emblem, of one saved soul, to another. It was in the quiet sense of having saved his souls that his deep strange instinct rejoiced. This was no dim theological rescue, no boon of a contingent world; they were saved better than faith or works could save them, saved for the warm world they had shrunk from dying to, for actuality, for continuity, for the certainty of human remembrance.

By this time he had survived all his friends; the last straight flame was three years old, there was no one to add to the list. Over and over he called his roll, and it appeared to him compact and complete. Where should he put in another, where, if there were no other objection, would it stand in its place in the rank? He reflected, with a want of sincerity of which he was quite conscious, that it would be difficult to determine that place. More and more, besides, face to face with his little legion, over endless histories, handling the empty shells and playing with the silence—more and more he could see that he had never introduced an alien. He had had his great companions, his indulgences—there were cases in which they had been immense; but what had his devotion after all been if it hadn't been at bottom a respect? He was, however, himself surprised at his stiffness; by the end of the winter the responsibility of it was what was uppermost in his thoughts. The refrain had grown old to them, that plea for just one more. There came a day when, for simple exhaustion, if symmetry should demand just one he was ready so far to meet symmetry. Symmetry was harmony, and the idea of harmony began to haunt him; he said to himself that harmony was of course everything. He took, in fancy, his composition to pieces, redistributing it into other lines, making other juxtapositions and contrasts. He shifted this and that candle, he made the spaces different, he effaced the disfigurement of a possible gap. There were subtle and complex relations, a scheme of cross-reference, and moments in which he seemed to catch a glimpse of the void so sensible to the woman who wandered in exile or sat where he had seen her with the portrait of Acton Hague. Finally, in this way, he arrived at a conception of the total, the ideal, which left a clear opportunity for just another figure. "Just one more—to round it off; just one more, just one," continued to hum in his head. There was a strange confusion in the thought, for he felt the day to be near when he too should be one of the Others. What in this event would the Others matter to him, since they only mattered to the living? Even as one of the Dead what would his altar matter to him, since his particular dream of keeping it up had melted away? What had harmony to do with the case if his lights were all to be quenched? What he had hoped for was an instituted thing. He might perpetuate it on some other pretext, but his special meaning would have dropped. This meaning was to have lasted with the life of the one other person who understood it.

In March he had an illness during which he spent a fortnight in bed, and when he revived a little he was told of two things that had happened. One was that a lady whose name was not known to the servants (she left none) had been three times to ask about him; the other was that in his sleep and on an occasion when his mind evidently wandered he was heard to murmur again and again: "Just one more—just one." As soon as he found himself able to go out, and before the doctor in attendance had pronounced him so, he drove to see the lady who had come to ask about him. She was not at home; but this gave him the opportunity, before his strength should fall again, to take his way to the church. He entered it alone; he had declined, in a happy manner he possessed of being able to decline effectively, the company of his servant or of a nurse. He knew now perfectly what these good people thought; they had discovered his clandestine connexion, the magnet that had drawn him for so many years, and doubtless attached a significance of their own to the odd words they had repeated to him. The nameless lady was the clandestine connexion—a fact nothing could have made clearer than his indecent haste to rejoin her. He sank on his knees before his altar while his head fell over on his hands. His weakness, his life's weariness overtook him. It seemed to him he had come for the great surrender. At first he asked himself how he should get away; then, with the failing belief in the power, the very desire to move gradually left him. He had come, as he always came, to lose himself; the fields of light were still there to stray in; only this time, in straying, he would never come back. He had given himself to his Dead, and it was good: this time his Dead would keep him. He couldn't rise from his knees; he believed he should never rise again; all he could do was to lift his face and fix his eyes on his lights. They looked unusually, strangely splendid, but the one that always drew him most had an unprecedented lustre. It was the central voice of the choir, the glowing heart of the brightness, and on this occasion it seemed to expand, to spread great wings of flame. The whole altar flared— dazzling and blinding; but the source of the vast radiance burned clearer than the rest, gathering itself into form, and the form was human beauty and human charity, was the far-off face of Mary Antrim. She smiled at him from the glory of heaven—she brought the glory down with her to take him. He bowed his head in submission and at the same moment another wave rolled over him. Was it the quickening of joy to pain? In the midst of his joy at any rate he felt his buried face grow hot as with some communicated knowledge that had the force of a reproach. It suddenly made him contrast that very rapture with the bliss he had refused to another. This breath of the passion immortal was all that other had asked; the descent of Mary Antrim opened his spirit with a great compunctious throb for the descent of Acton Hague. It was as if Stransom had read what her eyes said to him.

After a moment he looked round in a despair that made him feel as if the source of life were ebbing. The church had been empty—he was alone; but he wanted to have something done, to make a last appeal. This idea gave him strength for an effort; he rose to his feet with a movement that made him turn, supporting himself by the back of a bench. Behind him was a prostrate figure, a figure he had seen before; a woman in deep mourning, bowed in grief or in prayer. He had seen her in other days—the first time of his entrance there, and he now slightly wavered, looking at her again till she seemed aware he had noticed her. She raised her head and met his eyes: the partner of his long worship had come back. She looked across at him an instant with a face wondering and scared; he saw he had made her afraid. Then quickly rising she came straight to him with both hands out.

"Then you *could* come? God sent you!" he murmured with a happy smile.

"You're very ill—you shouldn't be here," she urged in anxious reply.

"God sent me too, I think. I was ill when I came, but the sight of you does wonders." He held her hands, which steadied and quickened him. "I've something to tell you."

"Don't tell me!" she tenderly pleaded; "let me tell you. This afternoon by a miracle, the sweetest of miracles, the sense of our difference left me. I was out—I was near, thinking, wandering alone, when, on the spot, something changed in my heart. It's my confession—there it is. To come back, to come back on the instant—the idea gave me wings. It was as if I suddenly saw something—as if it all became possible. I could come for what you yourself came for: that was enough. So here I am. It's not for my own—that's over. But I'm here for *them*." And breathless, infinitely relieved by her low precipitate explanation, she looked with eyes that reflected all its splendour at the magnificence of their altar.

"They're here for you," Stransom said, "they're present to-night as they've never been. They speak for you—don't you see?—in a passion of light; they sing out like a choir of angels. Don't you hear what they say?—they offer the very thing you asked of me."

"Don't talk of it—don't think of it; forget it!" She spoke in hushed supplication, and while the alarm deepened in her eyes she disengaged one of her hands and passed an arm round him to support him better, to help him to sink into a seat.

He let himself go, resting on her; he dropped upon the bench and she fell on her knees beside him, his own arm round her shoulder. So he remained an instant, staring up at his shrine. "They say there's a gap in the array—they say it's not full, complete. Just one more," he went on, softly—"isn't that what you wanted? Yes, one more, one more."

"Ah no more—no more!" she wailed, as with a quick new horror of it, under her breath.

"Yes, one more," he repeated, simply; "just one!" And with this his head dropped on her shoulder; she felt that in his weakness he had fainted. But alone with him in the dusky church a great dread was on her of what might still happen, for his face had the whiteness of death.

About Author

Henry James OM (15 April 1843 – 28 February 1916) was an American-British author regarded as a key transitional figure between literary realism and literary modernism, and is considered by many to be among the greatest novelists in the English language. He was the son of Henry James Sr. and the brother of renowned philosopher and psychologist William James and diarist Alice James.

He is best known for a number of novels dealing with the social and marital interplay between émigré Americans, English people, and continental Europeans. Examples of such novels include The Portrait of a Lady, The Ambassadors, and The Wings of the Dove. His later works were increasingly experimental. In describing the internal states of mind and social dynamics of his characters, James often made use of a style in which ambiguous or contradictory motives and impressions were overlaid or juxtaposed in the discussion of a character's psyche. For their unique ambiguity, as well as for other aspects of their composition, his late works have been compared to impressionist painting.

His novella The Turn of the Screw has garnered a reputation as the most analysed and ambiguous ghost story in the English language and remains his most widely adapted work in other media. He also wrote a number of other highly regarded ghost stories and is considered one of the greatest masters of the field.

James published articles and books of criticism, travel, biography, autobiography, and plays. Born in the United States, James largely relocated to Europe as a young man and eventually settled in England, becoming a British subject in 1915, one year before his death. James was nominated for the Nobel Prize in Literature in 1911, 1912 and 1916.

Life

Early years, 1843–1883

James was born at 2 Washington Place in New York City on 15 April 1843. His parents were Mary Walsh and Henry James Sr. His father was intelligent and steadfastly congenial. He was a lecturer and philosopher who had inherited independent means from his father, an Albany banker and investor. Mary came from a wealthy family long settled in New York City. Her sister Katherine lived with her adult family for an extended period of time. Henry Jr. had three brothers, William, who was one year his senior, and younger brothers Wilkinson (Wilkie) and Robertson. His younger sister was Alice. Both of his parents were of Irish and Scottish descent.

The family first lived in Albany, at 70 N. Pearl St., and then moved to Fourteenth Street in New York City when James was still a young boy. His education was calculated by his father to expose him to many influences, primarily scientific and philosophical; it was described by Percy Lubbock, the editor of his selected letters, as "extraordinarily haphazard and promiscuous." James did not share the usual education in Latin and Greek classics. Between 1855 and 1860, the James' household traveled to London, Paris, Geneva, Boulogne-sur-Mer and Newport, Rhode Island, according to the father's current interests and publishing ventures, retreating to the United States when funds were low. Henry studied primarily with tutors and briefly attended schools while the family traveled in Europe. Their longest stays were in France, where Henry began to feel at home and became fluent in French. He was afflicted with a stutter, which seems to have manifested itself only when he spoke English; in French, he did not stutter.

In 1860 the family returned to Newport. There Henry became a friend of the painter John La Farge, who introduced him to French literature, and in particular, to Balzac. James later called Balzac his "greatest master," and said that he had learned more about the craft of fiction from him than from anyone else.

In the autumn of 1861 Henry received an injury, probably to his back, while fighting a fire. This injury, which resurfaced at times throughout his life, made him unfit for military service in the American Civil War.

In 1864 the James family moved to Boston, Massachusetts to be near William, who had enrolled first in the Lawrence Scientific School at Harvard and then in the medical school. In 1862 Henry attended Harvard Law School, but realised that he was not interested in studying law. He pursued his interest in literature and associated with authors and critics William Dean Howells and Charles Eliot Norton in Boston and Cambridge, formed lifelong friendships with Oliver Wendell Holmes Jr., the future Supreme Court Justice, and with James and Annie Fields, his first professional mentors.

His first published work was a review of a stage performance, "Miss Maggie Mitchell in Fanchon the Cricket," published in 1863. About a year later, A Tragedy of Error, his first short story, was published anonymously. James's first payment was for an appreciation of Sir Walter Scott's novels, written for the North American Review. He wrote fiction and non-fiction pieces for The Nation and Atlantic Monthly, where Fields was editor. In 1871 he published his first novel, Watch and Ward, in serial form in the Atlantic Monthly. The novel was later published in book form in 1878.

During a 14-month trip through Europe in 1869–70 he met Ruskin, Dickens, Matthew Arnold, William Morris, and George Eliot. Rome impressed him profoundly. "Here I am then in the Eternal City," he wrote to his brother William. "At last—for the first time—I live!" He attempted to support himself as a freelance writer in Rome, then secured a position as Paris correspondent for the New York Tribune, through the influence of its editor John Hay. When these efforts failed he returned to New York City. During 1874 and 1875 he published Transatlantic Sketches, A Passionate Pilgrim, and Roderick Hudson. During this early period in his career he was influenced by Nathaniel Hawthorne.

In 1869 he settled in London. There he established relationships with Macmillan and other publishers, who paid for serial installments that they would later publish in book form. The audience for these serialized novels was largely made up of middle-class women, and James struggled to fashion serious literary work within the strictures imposed by editors' and publishers' notions of what was suitable for young women to read. He lived in rented rooms but was able to join gentlemen's clubs that had libraries and where he could entertain male friends. He was introduced to English society by Henry Adams and Charles Milnes Gaskell, the latter introducing him to the Travellers' and the Reform Clubs.

In the fall of 1875 he moved to the Latin Quarter of Paris. Aside from two trips to America, he spent the next three decades—the rest of his life—in Europe. In Paris he met Zola, Alphonse Daudet, Maupassant, Turgenev, and others. He stayed in Paris only a year before moving to London.

In England he met the leading figures of politics and culture. He continued to be a prolific writer, producing The American (1877), The Europeans (1878), a revision of Watch and Ward (1878), French Poets and Novelists (1878), Hawthorne (1879), and several shorter works of fiction. In 1878 Daisy Miller established his fame on both sides of the Atlantic. It drew notice perhaps mostly because it depicted a woman whose behavior is outside the social norms of Europe. He also began his first masterpiece, The Portrait of a Lady, which would appear in 1881.

In 1877 he first visited Wenlock Abbey in Shropshire, home of his friend Charles Milnes Gaskell whom he had met through Henry Adams. He was much inspired by the darkly romantic Abbey and the surrounding countryside, which features in his essay Abbeys and Castles. In particular the gloomy monastic fishponds behind the Abbey are said to have inspired the lake in The Turn of the Screw.

While living in London, James continued to follow the careers of the "French realists", Émile Zola in particular. Their stylistic methods influenced his own work in the years to come. Hawthorne's influence on him faded during this period, replaced by George Eliot and Ivan Turgenev. 1879–1882 saw the publication of The Europeans, Washington Square, Confidence, and The Portrait of a Lady. He visited America in 1882–1883, then returned to London.

The period from 1881 to 1883 was marked by several losses. His mother died in 1881, followed by his father a few months later, and then by his brother Wilkie. Emerson, an old family friend, died in 1882. His friend Turgenev died in 1883.

Middle years, 1884–1897

In 1884 James made another visit to Paris. There he met again with Zola, Daudet, and Goncourt. He had been following the careers of the French "realist" or "naturalist" writers, and was increasingly influenced by them. In 1886, he published The Bostonians and The Princess Casamassima, both influenced by the French writers he'd studied assiduously. Critical reaction and sales were poor. He wrote to Howells that the books had hurt his career rather than helped because they had "reduced the desire, and demand, for my productions to zero". During this time he became friends with Robert Louis Stevenson, John Singer Sargent, Edmund Gosse, George du Maurier, Paul Bourget, and Constance Fenimore Woolson. His third novel from the 1880s was The Tragic Muse. Although he was following the precepts of Zola in his novels of the '80s, their tone and attitude are closer to the fiction of Alphonse Daudet. The lack of critical and financial success for his novels during this period led him to try writing for the theatre. (His dramatic works and his experiences with theatre are discussed below.)

In the last quarter of 1889, he started translating "for pure and copious lucre" Port Tarascon, the third volume of Alphonse Daudet adventures of Tartarin de Tarascon. Serialized in Harper's Monthly Magazine from June 1890, this translation praised as "clever" by The Spectator was published in January 1891 by Sampson Low, Marston, Searle & Rivington.

After the stage failure of Guy Domville in 1895, James was near despair and thoughts of death plagued him. The years spent on dramatic works were not entirely a loss. As he moved into the last phase of his career he found ways to adapt dramatic techniques into the novel form.

In the late 1880s and throughout the 1890s James made several trips through Europe. He spent a long stay in Italy in 1887. In that year the short novel The Aspern Papers and The Reverberator were published.

Late years, 1898–1916

In 1897–1898 he moved to Rye, Sussex, and wrote The Turn of the Screw. 1899–1900 saw the publication of The Awkward Age and The Sacred

Fount. During 1902–1904 he wrote The Ambassadors, The Wings of the Dove, and The Golden Bowl.

In 1904 he revisited America and lectured on Balzac. In 1906–1910 he published The American Scene and edited the "New York Edition", a 24-volume collection of his works. In 1910 his brother William died; Henry had just joined William from an unsuccessful search for relief in Europe on what then turned out to be his (Henry's) last visit to the United States (from summer 1910 to July 1911), and was near him, according to a letter he wrote, when he died.

In 1913 he wrote his autobiographies, A Small Boy and Others, and Notes of a Son and Brother. After the outbreak of the First World War in 1914 he did war work. In 1915 he became a British subject and was awarded the Order of Merit the following year. He died on 28 February 1916, in Chelsea, London. As he requested, his ashes were buried in Cambridge Cemetery in Massachusetts.

Biographers

James regularly rejected suggestions that he should marry, and after settling in London proclaimed himself "a bachelor". F. W. Dupee, in several volumes on the James family, originated the theory that he had been in love with his cousin Mary ("Minnie") Temple, but that a neurotic fear of sex kept him from admitting such affections: "James's invalidism ... was itself the symptom of some fear of or scruple against sexual love on his part." Dupee used an episode from James's memoir A Small Boy and Others, recounting a dream of a Napoleonic image in the Louvre, to exemplify James's romanticism about Europe, a Napoleonic fantasy into which he fled.

Dupee had not had access to the James family papers and worked principally from James's published memoir of his older brother, William, and the limited collection of letters edited by Percy Lubbock, heavily weighted toward James's last years. His account therefore moved directly from James's childhood, when he trailed after his older brother, to elderly invalidism. As more material became available to scholars, including the diaries of contemporaries and hundreds of affectionate and sometimes erotic letters written by James to younger men, the picture of neurotic celibacy gave way to a portrait of a closeted homosexual.

Between 1953 and 1972, Leon Edel authored a major five-volume biography of James, which accessed unpublished letters and documents after Edel gained the permission of James's family. Edel's portrayal of James included the suggestion he was celibate. It was a view first propounded by critic Saul Rosenzweig in 1943. In 1996 Sheldon M. Novick published Henry James: The Young Master, followed by Henry James: The Mature Master (2007). The first book "caused something of an uproar in Jamesian circles" as it challenged the previous received notion of celibacy, a once-familiar paradigm in biographies of homosexuals when direct evidence was non-existent. Novick also criticised Edel for following the discounted Freudian interpretation of homosexuality "as a kind of failure." The difference of opinion erupted in a series of exchanges between Edel and Novick which were published by the online magazine Slate, with the latter arguing that even the suggestion of celibacy went against James's own injunction "live!"—not "fantasize!"

A letter James wrote in old age to Hugh Walpole has been cited as an explicit statement of this. Walpole confessed to him of indulging in "high jinks", and James wrote a reply endorsing it: "We must know, as much as possible, in our beautiful art, yours & mine, what we are talking about — & the only way to know it is to have lived & loved & cursed & floundered & enjoyed & suffered — I don't think I regret a single 'excess' of my responsive youth".

The interpretation of James as living a less austere emotional life has been subsequently explored by other scholars. The often intense politics of Jamesian scholarship has also been the subject of studies. Author Colm Tóibín has said that Eve Kosofsky Sedgwick's Epistemology of the Closet made a landmark difference to Jamesian scholarship by arguing that he be read as a homosexual writer whose desire to keep his sexuality a secret shaped his layered style and dramatic artistry. According to Tóibín such a reading "removed James from the realm of dead white males who wrote about posh people. He became our contemporary."

James's letters to expatriate American sculptor Hendrik Christian Andersen have attracted particular attention. James met the 27-year-old Andersen in Rome in 1899, when James was 56, and wrote letters to Andersen that are intensely emotional: "I hold you, dearest boy, in my innermost love, & count on your feeling me—in every throb of your soul". In a letter of 6 May 1904, to his brother William, James referred to himself as "always your hopelessly celibate even though sexagenarian Henry". How accurate that description might have been is the subject of contention among James's biographers, but the letters to Andersen were occasionally quasi-erotic: "I put, my dear boy, my arm around you, & feel the pulsation, thereby, as it were, of our excellent future & your admirable endowment." To his homosexual friend Howard Sturgis, James could write: "I repeat, almost to indiscretion, that I could live with you. Meanwhile I can only try to live without you."

His numerous letters to the many young gay men among his close male friends are more forthcoming. In a letter to Howard Sturgis, following a long visit, James refers jocularly to their "happy little congress of two" and in letters to Hugh Walpole he pursues convoluted jokes and puns about their relationship, referring to himself as an elephant who "paws you oh so benevolently" and winds about Walpole his "well meaning old trunk". His letters to Walter Berry printed by the Black Sun Press have long been celebrated for their lightly veiled eroticism.

He corresponded in almost equally extravagant language with his many female friends, writing, for example, to fellow novelist Lucy Clifford: "Dearest Lucy! What shall I say? when I love you so very, very much, and see you nine times for once that I see Others! Therefore I think that—if you want it made clear to the meanest intelligence—I love you more than I love Others." To his New York friend Mary Cadwalader Jones: "Dearest Mary Cadwalader. I yearn over you, but I yearn in vain; & your long silence really breaks my heart, mystifies, depresses, almost alarms me, to the point even of making me wonder if poor unconscious & doting old Célimare [Jones's pet name for James] has 'done' anything, in some dark somnambulism of the spirit, which has ... given you a bad moment, or a wrong impression, or a 'colourable pretext' ... However these things may be, he loves you as tenderly as ever;

174

nothing, to the end of time, will ever detach him from you, & he remembers those Eleventh St. matutinal intimes hours, those telephonic matinées, as the most romantic of his life ..." His long friendship with American novelist Constance Fenimore Woolson, in whose house he lived for a number of weeks in Italy in 1887, and his shock and grief over her suicide in 1894, are discussed in detail in Edel's biography and play a central role in a study by Lyndall Gordon. (Edel conjectured that Woolson was in love with James and killed herself in part because of his coldness, but Woolson's biographers have objected to Edel's account.)

Works

Style and themes

James is one of the major figures of trans-Atlantic literature. His works frequently juxtapose characters from the Old World (Europe), embodying a feudal civilisation that is beautiful, often corrupt, and alluring, and from the New World (United States), where people are often brash, open, and assertive and embody the virtues—freedom and a more highly evolved moral character—of the new American society. James explores this clash of personalities and cultures, in stories of personal relationships in which power is exercised well or badly. His protagonists were often young American women facing oppression or abuse, and as his secretary Theodora Bosanquet remarked in her monograph Henry James at Work:

> When he walked out of the refuge of his study and into the world and looked around him, he saw a place of torment, where creatures of prey perpetually thrust their claws into the quivering flesh of doomed, defenseless children of light ... His novels are a repeated exposure of this wickedness, a reiterated and passionate plea for the fullest freedom of development, unimperiled by reckless and barbarous stupidity.

Critics have jokingly described three phases in the development of James's prose: "James I, James II, and The Old Pretender." He wrote short stories and plays. Finally, in his third and last period he returned to the long, serialised novel. Beginning in the second period, but most noticeably in the third, he increasingly abandoned direct statement in favour of frequent

175

double negatives, and complex descriptive imagery. Single paragraphs began to run for page after page, in which an initial noun would be succeeded by pronouns surrounded by clouds of adjectives and prepositional clauses, far from their original referents, and verbs would be deferred and then preceded by a series of adverbs. The overall effect could be a vivid evocation of a scene as perceived by a sensitive observer. It has been debated whether this change of style was engendered by James's shifting from writing to dictating to a typist, a change made during the composition of What Maisie Knew.

In its intense focus on the consciousness of his major characters, James's later work foreshadows extensive developments in 20th century fiction. Indeed, he might have influenced stream-of-consciousness writers such as Virginia Woolf, who not only read some of his novels but also wrote essays about them. Both contemporary and modern readers have found the late style difficult and unnecessary; his friend Edith Wharton, who admired him greatly, said that there were passages in his work that were all but incomprehensible. James was harshly portrayed by H. G. Wells as a hippopotamus laboriously attempting to pick up a pea that had got into a corner of its cage. The "late James" style was ably parodied by Max Beerbohm in "The Mote in the Middle Distance".

More important for his work overall may have been his position as an expatriate, and in other ways an outsider, living in Europe. While he came from middle-class and provincial beginnings (seen from the perspective of European polite society) he worked very hard to gain access to all levels of society, and the settings of his fiction range from working class to aristocratic, and often describe the efforts of middle-class Americans to make their way in European capitals. He confessed he got some of his best story ideas from gossip at the dinner table or at country house weekends. He worked for a living, however, and lacked the experiences of select schools, university, and army service, the common bonds of masculine society. He was furthermore a man whose tastes and interests were, according to the prevailing standards of Victorian era Anglo-American culture, rather feminine, and who was shadowed by the cloud of prejudice that then and later accompanied suspicions of his homosexuality. Edmund Wilson famously compared James's objectivity to Shakespeare's:

One would be in a position to appreciate James better if one compared him with the dramatists of the seventeenth century—Racine and Molière, whom he resembles in form as well as in point of view, and even Shakespeare, when allowances are made for the most extreme differences in subject and form. These poets are not, like Dickens and Hardy, writers of melodrama—either humorous or pessimistic, nor secretaries of society like Balzac, nor prophets like Tolstoy: they are occupied simply with the presentation of conflicts of moral character, which they do not concern themselves about softening or averting. They do not indict society for these situations: they regard them as universal and inevitable. They do not even blame God for allowing them: they accept them as the conditions of life.

It is also possible to see many of James's stories as psychological thought-experiments. In his preface to the New York edition of The American he describes the development of the story in his mind as exactly such: the "situation" of an American, "some robust but insidiously beguiled and betrayed, some cruelly wronged, compatriot..." with the focus of the story being on the response of this wronged man. The Portrait of a Lady may be an experiment to see what happens when an idealistic young woman suddenly becomes very rich. In many of his tales, characters seem to exemplify alternative futures and possibilities, as most markedly in "The Jolly Corner", in which the protagonist and a ghost-doppelganger live alternative American and European lives; and in others, like The Ambassadors, an older James seems fondly to regard his own younger self facing a crucial moment.

Major novels

The first period of James's fiction, usually considered to have culminated in The Portrait of a Lady, concentrated on the contrast between Europe and America. The style of these novels is generally straightforward and, though personally characteristic, well within the norms of 19th-century fiction. Roderick Hudson (1875) is a Künstlerroman that traces the development of the title character, an extremely talented sculptor. Although the book shows some signs of immaturity—this was James's first serious attempt at a full-length novel—it has attracted favourable comment due to the vivid realisation of the three major characters: Roderick Hudson, superbly gifted but unstable and unreliable; Rowland Mallet, Roderick's limited but much more mature friend and patron; and Christina Light, one of James's most enchanting and maddening femmes fatales. The pair of Hudson and Mallet has been seen as representing the two sides of James's own nature: the wildly imaginative artist and the brooding conscientious mentor.

In The Portrait of a Lady (1881) James concluded the first phase of his career with a novel that remains his most popular piece of long fiction. The story is of a spirited young American woman, Isabel Archer, who "affronts her destiny" and finds it overwhelming. She inherits a large amount of money and subsequently becomes the victim of Machiavellian scheming by two American expatriates. The narrative is set mainly in Europe, especially in England and Italy. Generally regarded as the masterpiece of his early phase, The Portrait of a Lady is described as a psychological novel, exploring the minds of his characters, and almost a work of social science, exploring the differences between Europeans and Americans, the old and the new worlds.

The second period of James's career, which extends from the publication of The Portrait of a Lady through the end of the nineteenth century, features less popular novels including The Princess Casamassima, published serially in The Atlantic Monthly in 1885–1886, and The Bostonians, published serially in The Century Magazine during the same period. This period also featured James's celebrated Gothic novella, The Turn of the Screw.

The third period of James's career reached its most significant achievement in three novels published just around the start of the 20th century: The Wings of the Dove (1902), The Ambassadors (1903), and The Golden Bowl (1904). Critic F. O. Matthiessen called this "trilogy" James's major phase, and these novels have certainly received intense critical study. It was the second-written of the books, The Wings of the Dove (1902) that was the first published because it attracted no serialization. This novel tells the story of Milly Theale, an American heiress stricken with a serious disease, and her impact on the people around her. Some of these people befriend Milly with honourable motives, while others are more self-interested. James stated in his autobiographical books that Milly was based on Minny Temple, his beloved cousin who died at an early age of tuberculosis. He said that he attempted in the novel to wrap her memory in the "beauty and dignity of art".

Shorter narratives

James was particularly interested in what he called the "beautiful and blest nouvelle", or the longer form of short narrative. Still, he produced a number of very short stories in which he achieved notable compression of sometimes complex subjects. The following narratives are representative of James's achievement in the shorter forms of fiction.

- "A Tragedy of Error" (1864), short story
- "The Story of a Year" (1865), short story
- A Passionate Pilgrim (1871), novella
- Madame de Mauves (1874), novella
- Daisy Miller (1878), novella
- The Aspern Papers (1888), novella
- The Lesson of the Master (1888), novella
- The Pupil (1891), short story
- "The Figure in the Carpet" (1896), short story
- The Beast in the Jungle (1903), novella
- An International Episode (1878)
- Picture and Text
- Four Meetings (1885)
- A London Life, and Other Tales (1889)
- The Spoils of Poynton (1896)

- Embarrassments (1896)

- The Two Magics: The Turn of the Screw, Covering End (1898)

- A Little Tour of France (1900)

- The Sacred Fount (1901)

- Views and Reviews (1908)

- The Wings of the Dove, Volume I (1902)

- The Wings of the Dove, Volume II (1909)

- The Finer Grain (1910)

- The Outcry (1911)

- Lady Barbarina: The Siege of London, An International Episode and Other Tales (1922)

- The Birthplace (1922)

Plays

At several points in his career James wrote plays, beginning with one-act plays written for periodicals in 1869 and 1871 and a dramatisation of his popular novella Daisy Miller in 1882. From 1890 to 1892, having received a bequest that freed him from magazine publication, he made a strenuous effort to succeed on the London stage, writing a half-dozen plays of which only one, a dramatisation of his novel The American, was produced. This play was performed for several years by a touring repertory company and had a respectable run in London, but did not earn very much money for James. His other plays written at this time were not produced.

In 1893, however, he responded to a request from actor-manager George Alexander for a serious play for the opening of his renovated St. James's Theatre, and wrote a long drama, Guy Domville, which Alexander produced. There was a noisy uproar on the opening night, 5 January 1895, with hissing from the gallery when James took his bow after the final curtain, and the author was upset. The play received moderately good reviews and had a modest run of four weeks before being taken off to make way for Oscar Wilde's The Importance of Being Earnest, which Alexander thought would have better prospects for the coming season.

After the stresses and disappointment of these efforts James insisted that he would write no more for the theatre, but within weeks had agreed to write a curtain-raiser for Ellen Terry. This became the one-act "Summersoft", which he later rewrote into a short story, "Covering End", and then expanded into a full-length play, The High Bid, which had a brief run in London in 1907, when James made another concerted effort to write for the stage. He wrote three new plays, two of which were in production when the death of Edward VII on 6 May 1910 plunged London into mourning and theatres closed. Discouraged by failing health and the stresses of theatrical work, James did not renew his efforts in the theatre, but recycled his plays as successful novels. The Outcry was a best-seller in the United States when it was published in 1911. During the years 1890–1893 when he was most engaged with the theatre, James wrote a good deal of theatrical criticism and assisted Elizabeth Robins and others in translating and producing Henrik Ibsen for the first time in London.

Leon Edel argued in his psychoanalytic biography that James was traumatised by the opening night uproar that greeted Guy Domville, and that it plunged him into a prolonged depression. The successful later novels, in Edel's view, were the result of a kind of self-analysis, expressed in fiction, which partly freed him from his fears. Other biographers and scholars have not accepted this account, however; the more common view being that of F.O. Matthiessen, who wrote: "Instead of being crushed by the collapse of his hopes [for the theatre]... he felt a resurgence of new energy."

Non-fiction

Beyond his fiction, James was one of the more important literary critics in the history of the novel. In his classic essay The Art of Fiction (1884), he argued against rigid prescriptions on the novelist's choice of subject and method of treatment. He maintained that the widest possible freedom in content and approach would help ensure narrative fiction's continued vitality.

James wrote many valuable critical articles on other novelists; typical is his book-length study of Nathaniel Hawthorne, which has been the subject of critical debate. Richard Brodhead has suggested that the study was emblematic of James's struggle with Hawthorne's influence, and constituted an effort to place the elder writer "at a disadvantage." Gordon Fraser, meanwhile, has suggested that the study was part of a more commercial effort by James to introduce himself to British readers as Hawthorne's natural successor.

When James assembled the New York Edition of his fiction in his final years, he wrote a series of prefaces that subjected his own work to searching, occasionally harsh criticism.

At 22 James wrote The Noble School of Fiction for The Nation's first issue in 1865. He would write, in all, over 200 essays and book, art, and theatre reviews for the magazine.

For most of his life James harboured ambitions for success as a playwright. He converted his novel The American into a play that enjoyed modest returns in the early 1890s. In all he wrote about a dozen plays, most of which went unproduced. His costume drama Guy Domville failed disastrously on its opening night in 1895. James then largely abandoned his efforts to conquer the stage and returned to his fiction. In his Notebooks he maintained that his theatrical experiment benefited his novels and tales by helping him dramatise his characters' thoughts and emotions. James produced a small but valuable amount of theatrical criticism, including perceptive appreciations of Henrik Ibsen.

With his wide-ranging artistic interests, James occasionally wrote on the visual arts. Perhaps his most valuable contribution was his favourable assessment of fellow expatriate John Singer Sargent, a painter whose critical status has improved markedly in recent decades. James also wrote sometimes charming, sometimes brooding articles about various places he visited and lived in. His most famous books of travel writing include Italian Hours (an example of the charming approach) and The American Scene (most definitely on the brooding side).

James was one of the great letter-writers of any era. More than ten thousand of his personal letters are extant, and over three thousand have been published in a large number of collections. A complete edition of James's letters began publication in 2006, edited by Pierre Walker and Greg Zacharias. As of 2014, eight volumes have been published, covering the period from 1855 to 1880. James's correspondents included celebrated contemporaries like Robert Louis Stevenson, Edith Wharton and Joseph Conrad, along with many others in his wide circle of friends and acquaintances. The letters range from the "mere twaddle of graciousness" to serious discussions of artistic, social and personal issues.

Very late in life James began a series of autobiographical works: A Small Boy and Others, Notes of a Son and Brother, and the unfinished The Middle Years. These books portray the development of a classic observer who was passionately interested in artistic creation but was somewhat reticent about participating fully in the life around him.

Reception

Criticism, biographies and fictional treatments

James's work has remained steadily popular with the limited audience of educated readers to whom he spoke during his lifetime, and has remained firmly in the canon, but, after his death, some American critics, such as Van Wyck Brooks, expressed hostility towards James for his long expatriation and eventual naturalisation as a British subject. Other critics such as E. M. Forster complained about what they saw as James's squeamishness in the treatment of sex and other possibly controversial material, or dismissed his late style as difficult and obscure, relying heavily on extremely long sentences and excessively latinate language. Similarly Oscar Wilde criticised him for writing "fiction as if it were a painful duty". Vernon Parrington, composing a canon of American literature, condemned James for having cut himself off from America. Jorge Luis Borges wrote about him, "Despite the scruples and delicate complexities of James, his work suffers from a major defect: the absence of life." And Virginia Woolf, writing to Lytton Strachey, asked, "Please tell me what you find in Henry James. ... we have his works here, and

I read, and I can't find anything but faintly tinged rose water, urbane and sleek, but vulgar and pale as Walter Lamb. Is there really any sense in it?" The novelist W. Somerset Maugham wrote, "He did not know the English as an Englishman instinctively knows them and so his English characters never to my mind quite ring true," and argued "The great novelists, even in seclusion, have lived life passionately. Henry James was content to observe it from a window." Maugham nevertheless wrote, "The fact remains that those last novels of his, notwithstanding their unreality, make all other novels, except the very best, unreadable." Colm Tóibín observed that James "never really wrote about the English very well. His English characters don't work for me."

Despite these criticisms, James is now valued for his psychological and moral realism, his masterful creation of character, his low-key but playful humour, and his assured command of the language. In his 1983 book, The Novels of Henry James, Edward Wagenknecht offers an assessment that echoes Theodora Bosanquet's:

> "To be completely great," Henry James wrote in an early review, "a work of art must lift up the heart," and his own novels do this to an outstanding degree ... More than sixty years after his death, the great novelist who sometimes professed to have no opinions stands foursquare in the great Christian humanistic and democratic tradition. The men and women who, at the height of World War II, raided the secondhand shops for his out-of-print books knew what they were about. For no writer ever raised a braver banner to which all who love freedom might adhere.

William Dean Howells saw James as a representative of a new realist school of literary art which broke with the English romantic tradition epitomised by the works of Charles Dickens and William Makepeace Thackeray. Howells wrote that realism found "its chief exemplar in Mr. James... A novelist he is not, after the old fashion, or after any fashion but his own." F.R. Leavis championed Henry James as a novelist of "established pre-eminence" in The Great Tradition (1948), asserting that The Portrait of a Lady and The Bostonians were "the two most brilliant novels in the language." James is now prized as a master of point of view who moved literary fiction forward by insisting in showing, not telling, his stories to the reader. (Source: Wikipedia)

NOTABLE WORKS

NOVELS

Watch and Ward (1871)

Roderick Hudson (1875)

The American (1877)

The Europeans (1878)

Confidence (1879)

Washington Square (1880)

The Portrait of a Lady (1881)

The Bostonians (1886)

The Princess Casamassima (1886)

The Reverberator (1888)

The Tragic Muse (1890)

The Other House (1896)

The Spoils of Poynton (1897)

What Maisie Knew (1897)

The Awkward Age (1899)

The Sacred Fount (1901)

The Wings of the Dove (1902)

The Ambassadors (1903)

The Golden Bowl (1904)

The Whole Family (collaborative novel with eleven other authors, 1908)

The Outcry (1911)

The Ivory Tower (unfinished, published posthumously 1917)

The Sense of the Past (unfinished, published posthumously 1917)

SHORT STORIES AND NOVELLAS

A Tragedy of Error (1864)

The Story of a Year (1865)

A Landscape Painter (1866)

A Day of Days (1866)

My Friend Bingham (1867)

Poor Richard (1867)

The Story of a Masterpiece (1868)

A Most Extraordinary Case (1868)

A Problem (1868)

De Grey: A Romance (1868)

Osborne's Revenge (1868)

The Romance of Certain Old Clothes (1868)

A Light Man (1869)

Gabrielle de Bergerac (1869)

Travelling Companions (1870)

A Passionate Pilgrim (1871)

At Isella (1871)

Master Eustace (1871)

Guest's Confession (1872)

The Madonna of the Future (1873)

The Sweetheart of M. Briseux (1873)

The Last of the Valerii (1874)

Madame de Mauves (1874)

Adina (1874)

Professor Fargo (1874)

Eugene Pickering (1874)

Benvolio (1875)

Crawford's Consistency (1876)

The Ghostly Rental (1876)

Four Meetings (1877)

Rose-Agathe (1878, as Théodolinde)

Daisy Miller (1878)

Longstaff's Marriage (1878)

An International Episode (1878)

The Pension Beaurepas (1879)

A Diary of a Man of Fifty (1879)

A Bundle of Letters (1879)

The Point of View (1882)

The Siege of London (1883)

Impressions of a Cousin (1883)

Lady Barberina (1884)

Pandora (1884)

The Author of Beltraffio (1884)

Georgina's Reasons (1884)

A New England Winter (1884)

The Path of Duty (1884)

Mrs. Temperly (1887)

Louisa Pallant (1888)

The Aspern Papers (1888)

The Liar (1888)

The Modern Warning (1888, originally published as The Two Countries

A London Life (1888)

The Patagonia (1888)

The Lesson of the Master (1888)

The Solution (1888)

The Pupil (1891)

Brooksmith (1891)

The Marriages (1891)

The Chaperon (1891)

Sir Edmund Orme (1891)

Nona Vincent (1892)

The Real Thing (1892)

The Private Life (1892)

Lord Beaupré (1892)

The Visits (1892)

Sir Dominick Ferrand (1892)

Greville Fane (1892)

Collaboration (1892)

Owen Wingrave (1892)

The Wheel of Time (1892)

The Middle Years (1893)

The Death of the Lion (1894)

The Coxon Fund (1894)

The Next Time (1895)

Glasses (1896)

The Altar of the Dead (1895)

The Figure in the Carpet (1896)

The Way It Came (1896, also published as The Friends of the Friends)

The Turn of the Screw (1898)

Covering End (1898)

In the Cage (1898)

John Delavoy (1898)

The Given Case (1898)

Europe (1899)

The Great Condition (1899)

The Real Right Thing (1899)

Paste (1899)

The Great Good Place (1900)

Maud-Evelyn (1900)

Miss Gunton of Poughkeepsie (1900)

The Tree of Knowledge (1900)

The Abasement of the Northmores (1900)

The Third Person (1900)

The Special Type (1900)

The Tone of Time (1900)

Broken Wings (1900)

The Two Faces (1900)

Mrs. Medwin (1901)

The Beldonald Holbein (1901)

The Story in It (1902)

Flickerbridge (1902)

The Birthplace (1903)

The Beast in the Jungle (1903)

The Papers (1903)

Fordham Castle (1904)

Julia Bride (1908)

The Jolly Corner (1908)

The Velvet Glove (1909)

Mora Montravers (1909)

Crapy Cornelia (1909)

The Bench of Desolation (1909)

A Round of Visits (1910)

OTHER

Transatlantic Sketches (1875)

French Poets and Novelists (1878)

Hawthorne (1879)

Portraits of Places (1883)

A Little Tour in France (1884)

Partial Portraits (1888)

Essays in London and Elsewhere (1893)

Picture and Text (1893)

Terminations (1893)

Theatricals (1894)

Theatricals: Second Series (1895)

Guy Domville (1895)

The Soft Side (1900)

William Wetmore Story and His Friends (1903)

The Better Sort (1903)

English Hours (1905)

The Question of our Speech; The Lesson of Balzac. Two Lectures (1905)

The American Scene (1907)

Views and Reviews (1908)

Italian Hours (1909)

A Small Boy and Others (1913)

Notes on Novelists (1914)

Notes of a Son and Brother (1914)

Within the Rim (1918)

Travelling Companions (1919)

Notebooks (various, published posthumously)

The Middle Years (unfinished, published posthumously 1917)

A Most Unholy Trade (1925, published posthumously)

The Art of the Novel : Critical Prefaces (1934)